Sevyn

Lipstick & Leather Motorcycle Club

Emma Cole

The characters and events portrayed in this book are fictitious. Any similarity to real persons, living or dead, businesses, or locales is coincidental and is not intended by the author.

Cover Art – Everly Yours Cover Designs

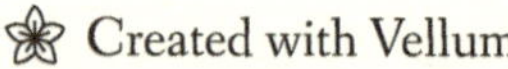

Cheers for women who know what they want and grab onto it with both hands.

Blurb

After a wild night with a pair of military men leaves Club President, Sevyn with an unexpected souvenir, she finds herself facing the responsibility alone. With a club to run, she juggles motherhood and leadership until a group of squatters infringe on her smuggling operation and ghosts return from the dead forcing her restructure her life.
Will our leading lady get the happily ever after she desires? Or will her world come crashing down around her?
Find out in Sevyn with adrenaline-pumping action and hotter romantic interactions that fill the pages in this gritty story of finding love and standing your ground.

Each book in the Lipstick & Leather Motorcycle Club is a standalone, contemporary reverse harem romance set in a shared world where ladies ride hard and shatter glass ceilings.

Content Warning

Mature/18+ only. Includes detailed steamy scenes including m/m, profanity, death, and other content that may not be suitable for all readers.

Alternate Character Names

Severine/Sevyn/Sevey/Prez – Club President
Florence/Aunt Flo/RagBag – Treasurer
Octavius Boudreaux/Gentry/Gus – Nomad
Lochlan Boudreaux/Loch – Nomad
Jessie O'Brien/Ares/Preppy – Nomad
Levi Thompson/Cooter/Coot – Nomad
Charlie/Tee – Vice President
Darius/Tank – Sgt-at-Arms
Brandon/Bronco/Bronc – Secretary
Althea/Jet – Road Captain
Albany/Dodo – Enforcer
Michael Brody/Doc – Tail Gunner/Chaplain
Nancy/Not Tanya – Club Whore

Chapter One

The rally grounds shook with the music pounding from the stage. It reverberated through my body, flaring the desire I already held in my core. I was celebrating tonight, and I had plans—plans that involved getting drunk and laid—and I didn't particularly care in what order they happened.

It was my last night before I took on the official mantle of the newest President of the Lipstick and Leather Motorcycle Club. I'd just received the approval for my petition to create the Montana chapter, so I had a package of patches in my toy hauler that would replace the black lips and 'nomad' on my jacket and those of my crew back home. But that was a task for tomorrow's Sevyn. Tonight was my last as a nomad, and I was going to make it one for the record books.

As I made my way through the crowd to the accompaniment of revving engines and rowdy party goers, I noticed two men that had caught my eye earlier during the rally. They kept popping up together, and at first I had thought they were a couple, despite their resemblance to one another, but I never saw them touch. Now, with another look, I figured they must be related. I wasn't sorry to admit that made my night, as I was more than a little attracted to them. They seemed to return the interest with the way they kept parallel to me, occasionally disappearing behind thick pockets of people and bikes, only to glance in my direction again when the crowd thinned as if to make sure I was still there.

I'd barely made it up to one of the bars, raising my voice over the din to ask for a snakebite with a beer chaser, when I felt the press and heat of a body against mine. I started to turn with a smile on my face, then froze when I saw two faces, one disappointed and the other plain pissed. But if they were over there, who the hell was behind me?

The guy was hot as fuck, I'd give him that, but I wasn't one to allow a man, or woman, to touch me without permission or at least a silent invitation...no matter the heat that burned in my belly.

"Excuse you, I think you've mistaken me for someone else," I informed the tall, shaggy-haired brunette with chocolate eyes and a dimple in his chin.

"Sure haven't, little lady," he shot back with a mischievous gleam in his eyes. I considered giving him a nudge out of my personal bubble, but was conscientious of the fact that although I wasn't wearing my new colors yet, I still had the responsibility of them. Getting into a bar fight with a dude a foot taller than me might be frowned upon unless he offered further provocation. "Sorry about plastering myself against your back. I only meant to get close enough so you could hear me, but I got bumped into."

Eyeing him suspiciously, I considered the truth of his words. He hadn't groped at me, and there was a sliver of space between us now, but I wasn't completely convinced it had been accidental.

"I'll have to take a raincheck. I already have plans," I finally answered, albeit a bit sharply in the tone arena. He was lucky he hadn't gotten worse for his little stunt, not that worse was off the table yet, but since he wore the same patches I, and the men who were closing in on us did, I would give him the benefit of the doubt until he proved otherwise. It wasn't uncommon for nomads of the same club to hook up since we tended to gravitate to each other during get-togethers like the rally, but invading my personal space was liable to get someone hurt if it was done purposely. And that sentiment wasn't just from me, it seemed. I watched the two men who had followed me split then come back together to bookend me, effectively trapping me between the three of them.

Before I could determine if shit was going to go down, a bang on the bar caused me to jump and crane my head over my shoulder, breaking the mesmerizing tableau. One of the dark-eyed, raven-haired duo smoothly set a hand on my hip, guiding me to finish my turn before releasing me, while his counterpart moved between me and the bubble-buster, forcing him to step back.

I kept half an ear out for what was being said while I paid the bartender and took the drinks he'd signaled me for, not that I could hear much unless they were shouting, and that wasn't happening yet. I wasn't the only one wanting to know what was going on, but gauging from the way the bartender eyed, then dismissed, the men behind me before moving along to another customer, they weren't going to have an altercation after all.

Taking a page from the bartender's book, I ignored the men behind me and slammed my shot, enjoying the sour kick to my tastebuds paired with the sweet burn of the honeyed whiskey. In contrast, the beer was ice-cold and took the edge off of the heat.

"Don't mind Coot. He likes to play games," my companion offered with a disarming grin.

Arching a brow as I glanced up at the man, I asked, "What kind of games does this *Coot* like to play?"

His grin widened into a full-blown smile before he held his hand out. "The kind where he tries to steal the hottest girl out from under us. I'm Loch, by the way, and my cousin over there is Gus, or Gentry if you prefer."

I took his hand, enjoying the way his rough callouses rasped against my own, though I was a bit surprised that he gave it a firm shake. Most men would squeeze too hard to assert their dominance or hold it like soiled tissue in a sissified pinch.

Deciding to be blunt and to the point as dusk was approaching, and I didn't want to be picking dudes with beer goggles on if either of these two didn't work out, I took a swig from the aluminum bottle, all that was allowed in the glass-free area, and blurted out, "Nice to meet you, Loch, but I'm kinda in the market for a hook-up with a side of small talk, not the other way around. So which one of you is interested?"

I swore his thought process slammed to a halt, and while he was rebooting, the band changed songs, letting me hear a groan come from where the other two were standing a few steps away.

"C'mon, Gus, give me a shot, too." With narrowed eyes, my head swiveled to level Coot with a glare. He instantly showed his palms, regret filling his eyes as he realized that I could hear him. "Sorry, ma'am," he apologized just as the next number started up.

It drowned out whatever Gus had to say to him, but with a dejected nod and a last glance my way, he turned and disappeared into the crowd. Strangely enough, considering the way he'd rubbed me wrong, I was kinda sad to see him go. Then my eyes fixated on the look-alike cousin while the other one, apparently ready to go again, leaned in close.

"We like to share, pretty lady. Do you think you're up for that?" He dropped the challenge like I'd be dropping my panties as soon as I had confirmation from his cousin...and a few more drinks in me.

Apparently, said cousin had heard him, or he could lip read, because he winked as he sidled up next to me. "We'd love nothing more than to rock your world, but I'd like to know your name first, if you don't mind?"

"Sevyn, but feel free to improvise when I'm on your dick, riding into the dawn," I retorted, giving him a smirk before I downed my beer and yelled for another round.

~

"Oh, fuck me," I groaned, chin on my chest, lids at half-mast as I gripped Gus' short dark hair in my fist and ground my pussy harder against his face. I was nearly there. The suction and flicking tongue to my clit were about to do me in if I had just a minute more, but then I was reminded that my other partner had only retreated to suit up. He brushed against my back, breaking my concentration.

"I plan to, darlin', just as soon as you scoot that fine ass back here." Loch's promise rumbled in my ear an instant before his hands gripped my hips to pull me back, unearthing his cousin's glistening cheeks, until I knelt between Gus' thighs, my hands on either side of his hips. "So fucking wet for us," Loch praised before sinking two fingers deep into my clenching channel.

My lips parted in a gasp of pure pleasure right

over the thick and rigid pole of flesh, the reddened tip graced by a shiny drop of precum. I worked my hips in tandem with the rhythm of the hand between my legs, watching in rapt attention as Gus gripped his length, arching up to paint my lips with the evidence of his desire. Darting my tongue out, I dipped it into the damp slit before swirling it around the crest of his dick, earning a groan in response.

"Hurry up, Lochlan, or I'm going to let her ride my dick like she rode my face, and you'll have to wait your turn," Gus warned his cousin, his voice as strained as the erection he held in a death grip. But I had no intent to make him wait his turn to get off. I adjusted my position to get a better angle for the blow job I planned to give him, which also happened to arch my back and lift my ass as if I were a presenting bitch in heat. Not that that was far off from the way I was feeling right then.

"Hold your horses," Loch griped back, pulling his fingers from me then gripping my hip with the same hand, his fingers wet against my skin, as I felt his other arm brush against my inner thighs, guiding his dick to my entrance.

The broad head briefly paused in its attempt at entry while my body tried to adjust to let him in. The burn of his entry was enough to pierce through my buzz, turning into a special kind of ecstasy as his body thrust into my slick depths. The cry that left my throat was full of surprise at how good it felt, and Gus' knowing gaze met mine as I clenched around his cousin when he bottomed out.

"Is your world rocking yet?" Gus teased, steadily stroking a dick slightly thinner than the one filling me to the brim. Fuckers hadn't let me get a look at it beforehand, and I'd figured Lochlan was smaller since he was going first. Would teach me to assume shit. My world *was* rocking, but it wasn't only from the skilled thrusts well on their way to making me see stars.

With a smirk I was proud to manage, I snarked back, "Of course it's rocking. We're going at it in a toy hauler—" My words cut off in a gasp as a trail of pure heat ran up my middle.

"I think you found the spot," Gus informed his cousin, who nailed said spot again hard enough that I could feel the flesh of my ass and thighs shudder from the impact. Not to mention what it did to my free-hanging breasts, something Gus was quick to take advantage of. He managed to stretch enough to catch the peaks between his fingers, the pinch as they slipped away garnering a moan from me.

He wasn't wrong about Lochlan's technique, though, and I dove onto his dick to muffle the sounds I knew I couldn't hold back. I let him fill my mouth until he hit the end, then he slipped down my throat with a little effort from me, his groan joining the sharp slaps of skin-on-skin and noises of pleasure as we sought to bring each other to completion.

Another dozen thrusts in, I was screaming around Gus' dick, and moments later, they reached their own peaks. One flooded my mouth with the salty taste of cum while my grasping pussy tried to pull the other throbbing length deeper as if it never wanted to let him go. A deep and satisfied chuckle sounded out behind me while I cleaned every trace of cum from Gus' waning erection. His hand came up to caress my cheek, affection shining from his dark eyes as his thumb traced my swollen lips.

"I think I could get used to this," he said softly, his tone and expression indicating he was interested in more than just being fuck buddies.

His cousin was of the same mind, which wasn't a surprise given that they had said they liked to share right off the bat. "Can't say I disagree with you, if Sevyn here is amenable."

Loch's grip on my hips loosened from where I'd surely have imprints from his fingertips in the morning, reminders of my wild night that had the potential to become more. There was a major problem though. As far as they knew, I was a nomad, happy to travel wherever the road took me.

But I wasn't a wandering member; I'd just taken up the mantle of leadership for my own club. Before I could broach the subject, odd as it was to have the conversation in our respective positions, and nude, Loch put another damper on the moment. "We'll be gone a while, but we'll get in touch when we get back, if you're still interested, that is."

When I twisted my head, the regret in his eyes had me wondering what I wasn't getting, but Gus distracted me by sitting up and pulling me over him. His lips took mine in a fierce kiss, one hand seeking out a nipple to tease while the other settled between my legs to work its magic.

"Let's discuss after we've all had our fill and made sure you never forget us. Hopefully, that'll convince you to give us a chance." Gus' voice, while husky with lust, was just as filled with determination, and I had a feeling once he set his sights on something, his mind was made up. He wouldn't take no for an answer without a hell of a fight. The prospect was one I looked forward to despite the unorthodox arrangement the three of us would make.

The rest of the night was spent in a tangle of limbs with so many orgasms I wasn't sure I'd be able to sit on my bike for a week without feeling the aftershocks. As far as convincing went, they did a bang-up job of it.

The rasp of stubble against my cheek had me turning my head to bury it further into my pillow with a groan. There was no way I was up for another round. I was worn the fuck out and needed several more hours of sleep. Whichever one of the guys it was, gently pulled my hair back to kiss his way down my neck. When he reached the area between my neck and shoulder, he sucked hard before letting off with a pop. Instantly, I lifted my head to glare into Gus' face.

A deep laugh preceded the words I wasn't at all interested in hearing. "Morning, pretty lady. We have to go and didn't want to leave without telling you goodbye—and without giving you something to remember us by." His finger traced over what had to be one heck of a hickey, but I couldn't stay irritated about it when he put it that way. It wasn't like I had anyone to answer to about the mark. Hell, half the girls back home regularly sported them like badges of honor.

Voice husky from sleep and overuse of my vocal chords from the rowdy night, I asked the most important question. "How long do you plan on being out of reach?"

A shadow passed over his eyes as Loch made

room for himself on the edge of the bed. Staring between them, I got the gist that I wasn't going to like the answer.

"That's not something I can give you a concrete answer on. We're part of a specialized unit under an offshoot branch of the military." Gus paused and glanced at his cousin, who shook his head with a shrug. I was pretty sure Loch had just declined to take over, but I couldn't be certain until Gus sighed and continued on. "There are a few years left on our contract. We reupped six months ago and have been on leave the last couple weeks. We're due to report in tomorrow and need to handle the last few details like storing our bikes and making the drive to base, so we have to get going this morning. We'll leave you our phone numbers, and I hope you'll give us yours, but we won't be able to use them until we're back stateside." He shut up at a sharp glance from Loch, and I had to wonder just who I'd spent the night with.

"Gus is feeling guilty and pissed that we have to leave so soon after meeting you. I can't blame him since I'm not so fond of the idea myself. I'd much rather be in bed with you, but he's bound to overshare what we're allowed to if I let him keep on. We get leave about every four to six months, give or take a few weeks, depending on what our assignment is. If we get a chance, we'll get in touch sooner, even if it's just to send a quick message, and you can do the same. Neither of us want to lose out on a chance with you, and we'll promise now that there won't be any other women until we've had an opportunity to explore what might be between us. Will you do the same?"

This Lochlan was much more to the point and no-nonsense than the charmer from last night, and I thought it likely had something to do with his impending return to what had to be a strict structure and routine. But right then, I had his full attention while he waited on my answer. Feeling somewhat defensive that my plans for a one-night stand hadn't quite panned out as planned, on top of my insecurity over catching feelings, I almost snarked back at him. Instead, I held my tongue, they were being straight with me; I could return the favor.

"I'll wait for you to touch base, but since we're being all transparent and shit, I have to tell you that yesterday was officially my last as a nomad. I'm the newest chapter president...in Charity Falls, Montana." I winced at naming my home state clear across the country, but neither of them looked a bit surprised.

"We weren't snooping," he was quick to inform me with his hands up. "The flaps weren't closed all the way, and we were trying to quietly hunt our clothes down without waking you up. I'm glad you told us, though. We can discuss it when we get back. I'm not opposed to giving the northwest a go as long as Gus isn't."

The man in question shrugged, then hesitated. "I'm not, but we might have to talk the others into it." His answer was more to Loch than to me, so I held my curiosity as to who the 'others' were. I wanted to know everything about them, but I knew that there plain wasn't time for it right then.

"It's a deal then," I confirmed before sitting up and letting the blanket pool around my waist, exposing my chest, as I reached for my phone. The slight heat of a blush worked across my cheeks at the appreciative stares despite them having been up close and personal with most of my anatomy last night.

I opened my phone and handed it off for them to add their contacts while I went pee and brushed my teeth in the tiny bathroom. And then it was down to minutes before they had to go.

An ache formed in my chest after they both kissed me goodbye and disappeared from sight while I watched from the open door of the tiny trailer still filled with the scent of them. I wanted to call them back, ask them not to leave, but I knew they couldn't stay, no matter how my intuition beat at me to do so.

Instead, I started packing up, procrastinating on a shower until I had nothing left to do because I didn't want to wash them off of me.

Finally, I had my bike strapped in, the toy hauler hitched to my truck, and I was ready to begin the long drive home.

Chapter Two

2 Months Later

"Well, Sevey, what do they say?" came Aunt Flo's voice through the bathroom door. "Don't leave me hanging out here, girl. Do you need help? Did you read the instructions?"

I barely registered what she was saying as I stared at the counter with a line of three white sticks, all saying the same thing. *Pregnant.* My mind raced back to that night at the rally, then to the trash can I'd emptied the next day. "But we used condoms," I whispered to myself. And then louder, "I'm on fucking birth control!"

After my outburst, my aunt didn't wait to come in. The door opened as I turned to dry heave over the toilet, though strings of saliva and stomach acid were all that came out. I had hardly been able to eat a damn thing in over a week. That was what prompted my decision to take the tests.

"Oh, Sevey, honey," my aunt comforted while rubbing small circles on my back. "Whatever you want to do, I support you a hundred percent. If you want to keep this baby, I'll be there like I was for your mama. If not, I'll hold your hand the entire time."

Leave it to Aunt Flo to get to the root of it right off the bat. I wasn't ready. I wasn't sure if I would ever be ready, not after Mama hemorrhaged and died while trying to have my baby sister, taking them both from me in less than an hour. I'd only been five, but I remembered that day vividly. I'd always been meticulous about making sure my ass was covered so I wouldn't end up with an accidental pregnancy.

Gaining my composure as I stood and flushed the toilet, I went to the sink to rinse my mouth out and opened the vanity drawer to sweep the sticks into it before slamming it closed again. Out of sight wasn't out of mind in this case, but I couldn't stand to look at them any longer. My aunt patiently waited until I turned and leaned against the counter with a sigh.

"I have no clue what I'm going to do. Can I even handle being pregnant while running the club and the bar? How the hell does a *baby* fit into this lifestyle? The members that have kids don't bring them around except on family days or when they know other shit isn't going down. I don't *have* that option." An inarticulate scream muffled behind closed lips finished off the handful of issues that came to mind right off. Who knew what else would crop up. An outlaw biker club wasn't the place to raise a baby.

"First things first—give it a few days and let the news settle. You don't have to make any decisions right now. There are some dos and don'ts, but we can look those up and then you can decide. In the meantime, we have church tonight. This'll still be waiting when you're ready." Aunt Flo paused as she opened the door to my bedroom, looking over her shoulder before adding, "And maybe consider contacting the father? He might want some input, too." She left, presumably to start preparations for the meeting, but I knew that Mama not telling my father, whoever he was, about me, had never sat right with my aunt.

I had no intention of *not* telling Gus or Lochlan, but getting in touch with them wasn't going to be easy. I'd be the one making the decision before they even knew. There wasn't any way around that.

With another sigh, I shut the bathroom light out and crossed my bedroom, ready to head down the lane to the Hideaway. My bar, as well as the attached clubhouse, had extra rooms upstairs for club members and was located a ways away from the house on my property.

The Hideaway was more than a local biker bar though. It was a convenient front to distribute our product, an item on tonight's agenda, while helping to facilitate the other aspect of our operation...black market WITSEC. Neither topic could afford distraction, so I had to get my head on straight and attend to them.

~

Six Months Later

"Come on, why the hell aren't they answering?" I grumbled for the third time that week when Gus' phone went straight to voicemail again. A *full* voice mailbox. Scrolling through my text messages, I went back to the ones he and Lochlan had sent me before they shipped out.

Loch had sent a pic Gus took during the night we spent together; we were both up on our knees, my back to his chest and my head tipped back on his shoulders, with our lips fused together and his hands gripping my breasts. The caption reminded me not to forget about him. There were two from Gus—one of the three of us, mussed and worn out, me snuggled in between them. The other was a promise to get in touch when they could, that they'd found out their assignment would be a bit longer than usual.

Yet the time frame, plus some, had come and gone, and there was still nothing from them. I was nearly out of time to inform them that one of them was about to be a father since my due date was in six weeks. Glancing down at my baby beach ball, I rubbed the swell of my stomach then winced as the little miss ground her head into what felt like the entirety of my pelvic bones. The urge to pee was immediate, but I wanted to try Loch's number before I waddled to the toilet *again*.

When I hit send, I fully expected to get the same result as Gus', but the vacant number tone came through the speaker along with the 'this number is no longer in service' message. My heart dropped before it started racing, a sense of dread filling me. *Why would his phone be shut off?* I tried it again in case it was a mix-up and got the same result. Scenarios ran through my head, from him not paying his bill to having the number deliberately changed. I didn't know much at all about either of them, other than they knew how to use their dicks, and they had *said* they were interested in more. I really had to consider that they'd lost interest and this was at least Lochlan's way of moving on.

Before my paranoid, pregnant brain could devise any other wild thoughts about getting played, I sent a text to Gus' phone, telling him I needed to speak to him immediately and to call as soon as possible. Trying to put my concerns out of mind, I left my phone on the bed and went to use the bathroom. I was just washing my hands when I heard the chiming of my ringtone and hurried as much as I could to find Gus' name lighting up the screen.

Relief filled me, as well as a hefty dose of anger, that he was finally bothering to return my calls. All it took was an emergent message, and that didn't sit well with me. Swiping to accept the call, I started in before he could even offer a greeting, then realized the line was dead. Instantly, I hit the call back button and tapped my foot impatiently as I waited for him to answer. Except it went straight to his voicemail again. Beyond pissed and hurt, I sent another message, this one containing a video taken in my mirror highlighting my swollen stomach.

The phone lit up with an incoming call a second after the message showed it had been opened.

"Dude, what the fuck? I know you said it would be a few months, but sometimes shit is time sensitive, and I shouldn't have to say it's an emergency to get a call back." I stopped to take a breath; kicking baby feet and the swell of my uterus pressing on my diaphragm and lungs really took the wind out of me...literally.

"I'm sorry, but you're yelling at the wrong person, ma'am. I didn't mean to call the first time. It was an accident when I opened the message. I went to shut it off, but the video came in, then I saw your picture matched the background, and... Look, I'm only housekeeping, and I can get into a lot of shit for telling you anything, but obviously you haven't been informed, and it's important." The man paused, and I took the opportunity to cut in.

"Where's Gus? And Lochlan, his phone was disconnected. Obviously, you know more than a random housekeeper, buddy. How did you get past the lock screen if you're *just* a housekeeper?" The guy didn't sound like either Lochlan or Gus, but they'd said there were others. For all I knew, this was his way of ditching out after seeing I was pregnant. It sounded far-fetched, even to myself, so I braced myself to hear they'd been thrown in jail or something, but I wasn't at all prepared for what he had to say.

"I'm sorry, ma'am. There's a protocol to follow, and 'housekeeper' is as much as I'm willing to offer. Sergeant Major Boudreaux's team is MIA and presumed to be deceased. Their plane went down on their last mission and was unrecoverable. That's all I know and more than I should have shared, but I wouldn't want my girlfriend to wonder what happened with a baby on the way. Good luck, ma'am, I wish you the best." He didn't wait for a reply before hanging up, leaving me standing there in disbelief.

My frequent fantasies had featured a reunion where both men were surprised but happy to have me and the baby, but those fantasies shattered into a thousand pieces as I crumpled onto the bed, cradling my stomach, as the tears came. There would never be *any* reaction, good or bad, for the little girl I carried. I didn't even know which man had fathered her, or if they had family that might want to know her.

I laid there, sobbing my heart out for both of us—me for losing what could have been, and her, for having to go through life without a dad. I knew how that was first hand. Aunt Flo had been amazing, but I was an orphan, my aunt my only family, and now we were all my baby had.

Some time later, my aunt came in search of me, alarm in her voice as she shook my arm. "Severine! What happened?!"

Groggily, I sat up, realizing that I'd fallen asleep at some point. "They're gone," I rasped, throat scratchy as hell. My vocal chords were probably as swollen as my eyes felt, and I knew my face had to be blotchy too.

"Who's gone? I came up here and thought you'd passed out! Scared the life outta me, child."

"The men...one of them was the baby's father." My voice broke as I teared up again, but I pushed through it, recounting almost robotically the events from earlier. "I've been trying to get in touch with them for months. They were part of some specialized military unit, and their plane went down. The man that answered Gus' phone said they're MIA and presumed dead."

Sympathy filled my aunt's eyes as she sat next to me and pulled me in for a hug. I didn't think she'd quite believed I had attempted to contact them; she'd asked twice if I wanted to request their membership information to get in touch. There had been no judgment that there were two of them, no, my aunt had been amused with that revelation, but she'd been urging me more and more to let them know before the baby arrived.

"I'm so sorry, Sevey. Are you sure it wasn't someone playing a shitty joke? I know you've been hesitant to request the member records, but we could check, just in case?"

I didn't think the man had been lying, but it wouldn't hurt to ask, and maybe they had next-of-kin listed that might be interested in knowing the baby. A tiny bit of hope tried to grow as I agreed to give it a shot. Needing to pee, I scooted to the edge of the bed, but as I went to push myself up, my bladder gave up.

"Motherfucker, now I have to shower and change the bed." My embarrassment was loud and clear, but my aunt was shaking her head before I made it two steps.

"Honey, urine doesn't gush like that. I'm pretty sure your water just broke."

The blood rushed from my face fast enough to leave me lightheaded. It was too early for the baby to come now.

"No, no. No passing out on me," my aunt admonished, correctly interpreting my expression. "It's only a few weeks, and the hospital isn't too far. Let's just think happy thoughts and get there." She gave me a pep talk as she got up and bustled me off to the bathroom. "You take a *quick* shower, and I'll get our bags and let Tee know he's in charge until further notice. Hurry up, now. I'm not delivering a baby on the highway. Besides, you'll want the drugs." The last bit was muttered as she took off to handle packing the car and tell my VP that I was going to be out of commission for a few days.

My concern came back in full force despite Aunt Flo's positivity. I didn't want to lose them *and* her. My heart couldn't take it.

Nearly eight hours later, Opal Luna Boudreaux was born. A bit on the small side but healthy nonetheless. I'd contemplated giving her my surname, Delaney, but when Aunt Flo got confirmation from the mother chapter, I'd figured I could at least give them, and her, that much. The day was bittersweet, but I vowed to be everything my daughter needed in life, no matter how hard it was.

Chapter Three

Two Years Later

"What about our suppliers? How is that going to affect our relationship with them if we go legit?" My gangly, bearded secretary was about on my last nerve with this damn argument. He was like a broken record, repeating the same shit because he didn't like change. Brandon, or Bronco as he preferred to go by, had been against building our own above-board operation after pot was legalized in the state. He didn't think it was worth having it overseen by the state government when we had a smooth and lucrative operation set up already. But I felt we were missing a huge opportunity to make more money without all of the risk.

"They're fine with it. I already handled that end of things and set them up with another interested party." The uproar was immediate, even from the more level-headed club members.

"What the fuck, Prez? I thought we were waiting on a vote. I'm with Bronc on this one. I don't want our business outed should the law change again, but you also should have waited for everyone's input instead of making an executive decision." Most of my crew agreed with my VP, but they were missing one thing Tee hadn't bothered to bring up.

"Why are there still fucking squatters spreading their camp and trash out on the strip of land between us and our drop point then, Charlie? As my vice president, you were supposed to handle relocating them without drawing attention or blowing up our operation. When I told our suppliers we'd have to make a new drop point, and *why*, they were less than amused." I spread my hands, inviting him to answer, but of course he couldn't, which turned most of the irritation from me to Tee. Normally, I wouldn't have thrown his ass under the bus, but we'd gone round and round this shit for the last two meetings, and if we were going to go legit, I needed to file the paperwork with the state, asap. Besides...

"Charlie, we go way back, and you've been there when I needed you, but don't forget the land, my house that sits on it, and the bar are mine. We all chose to build onto the bar instead of buying or renting something else for the clubhouse, but I won't have my home or business seized because of some pissant squatters narcing us out or fucking around and causing us to get caught."

Tee backed down, still pissed, but he was unable to argue with my logic or my edict. Ultimately, the final say was mine, and I was using that option now.

"What are we going to do in the meantime so our supply chain isn't interrupted?" Bronco asked, cautiously this time.

"What do you want me to do, Sevey? I can't just force them out. They're on public land. When I tried to get them to relocate, they complained that a lot of their old spots have been bought up by developers, so they'd been run off. Unless you want to buy the land they're sitting on, there isn't much recourse." Tee's frustration was palpable, but so was mine, and I was irritated on top of it.

"I expected that you could get creative, but I guess that's not happening. Let's move on before this derails the meeting and ends up in a fight, yeah?" It was about the only compromise I was willing to offer since letting my VP dictate to me wasn't exactly a good look for the club president. Tee shut up, but from his glare, he was just as happy as I was with the disagreement.

"What are we going to do in the meantime so our supply chain isn't interrupted?" Bronco asked, cautiously this time, helpfully moving the meeting along.

"Actually, I want you to head that up with Aunt Flo. You two get together, grab the prospects if you need to, and figure out the best setup for hydroponics and one of those prefab buildings. We'll get started in there for the year-round shit, and Tank and Jet can begin preparing the clear cut and the meadow. We won't be able to hit the growing season this year, even if we had the approval today, but we can be prepared for spring. And, Jet," I continued, turning my attention to the svelte road captain, "start planning our last club ride of the season. Once the temps start dropping, it'll be too dangerous to chance running into ice or snow."

Jet, aka Althea, nodded as she held up two fingers while the burly sergeant-at-arms, Tank, barked out, "Got it."

Wanting to wrap the meeting up, but also give my crew a chance to come to terms with the decision after blindsiding them, I left the floor open to discussion. While they talked amongst themselves, I checked in on Opal, sleeping in the room I kept for myself above the clubhouse and bar. Her dark curls were strewn across the pillow, and she clutched at her favorite blanket that was starting to look on the ratty side. With her rose and porcelain complexion and pouty lips just begging for me to sneak in and take pictures, I had a hard time pulling my attention back to the meeting.

"Alright, guys, let's wrap it up if there isn't anything pertinent to discuss. We all know what's on the agenda for the foreseeable future, and if you have issues, you know where to find Sevyn." Aunt Flo, forever having my back, got the room under control in an instant.

Tee, looking contrite, relented on the squatter issue. "I'll go up to their camp again. I warned them about the property line, poaching, and tried to scare them off a bit, but I can't exactly threaten them."

With a sigh, I had to admit he was right; violence would only bring on an investigation, and as we still had a few runs to make across the border, we couldn't afford the scrutiny. "Fine, we'll touch base on the subject at our next meeting. I'm hoping they'll pack up when the weather turns anyway." He nodded with no further comment.

After I gave a cursory glance around to make sure no one else wanted to speak up, I slapped the gavel on the table with a "Church dismissed," then waited for everyone to file out. I felt a headache brewing behind my eyes, likely from juggling the stress of the summer and the abrupt change in plans that had to be made since the group of vagabonds had started setting up camp.

"Hey, Sevey? You got a minute?" My eyes popped open to find Dodo, my blond, shaggy-headed enforcer, standing in front of the table.

"Yeah, sure, what's up?" I stood from my seat, giving the baby monitor a quick check before Aunt Flo held her hand out to me. With a grateful tip of my head, I handed the monitor over, knowing I could concentrate on club business and wouldn't need to worry about Opal until I went upstairs to relieve my aunt.

"Sheriff called, said he wanted to stop by in the morning. He has a party of three that he thinks needs our help."

My headache was instantly pushed to the side as I focused on what would throw us all in jail for many, many years if it were ever found out—identity forging. We specialized in helping families in need disappear from abusive or dangerous situations when the law had their hands tied. We also manufactured documentation for others on the mother chapter's request in exchange for the supplies needed to do it.

"I'm assuming they have a safe place to stay tonight?" Dodo nodded and held out a piece of scrap paper with enough information scribbled on it to get me started. "I'll get on these tonight and send the sheriff a message. Thanks for taking the call. I probably have my ringer off from getting Opal down." I thought that was it, but he didn't move, prompting me to ask, "Was there more?"

It was unlike the usual no-nonsense enforcer to be hesitant, but then I caught the look in his eyes and nearly rolled my own. Ever since I weaned the baby a couple months ago, several of the club members had hit on me, as if the lack of a kid attached to my tits was the neon 'open' sign they'd been waiting for. Hell, even Theo, the sheriff, had shown interest. Though, to be fair, he'd never *not* shown interest, but he was an ex-boyfriend from high school, and I wasn't sure I wanted to go that route again.

As for the club members... I'd gone so long without getting laid that it seemed wrong to start sleeping around and muddy the waters. Besides, between the club whores and prospects, there was plenty of ass to choose from as long as they were all amenable, which they usually were.

"I was thinking maybe since Flo has Miss Opal, you'd like to go for a ride and get something to eat? I saw you rubbing at your temples. Some fresh air might help with that sore head. Or I could give you a massage in private..." He trailed off at the death glare I shot him.

"Albany, I've made it more than clear that I'm not interested in a quick fuck or dating right now, especially within the club. That's just asking for trouble we don't need. I don't want to be a bitch because I respect you, but I want some of that same respect, and you ignoring what I've said puts me in a shitty position. You're my enforcer. You're the one that's supposed to *enforce* the club rules. What the hell am I supposed to do if you're skirting them?"

Hands held up in surrender, he played as if he were shocked, though I knew he was smarter than he was acting. "It was just an offer, Sevey, didn't mean to rile you up. I'll head on out and make sure Bronco isn't 'taking advantage' of the prospects," he nearly snapped at me before turning on his heel and stalking out. The man was hot in a grungy way, and a few years ago, I'd have been happy to climb that tree, but this was my home as much as it was my livelihood, and I couldn't see jeopardizing that over a hook-up. Not when I had Opal to consider.

But I also didn't care for the way he'd talked to me, so I stormed out after him with half a mind to chew his ass in public for flipping me attitude. Of course, I ran smack dab into the middle of rowdy bikers surrounding a table where two of the ladies that liked to hang around had each other's skirts hiked up with their heads buried between the other's legs.

Money was changing hands lightning quick, and I knew Bronco had to be behind the betting. He liked to pit the women, or men, against each other to see who could make the other get off first. The one that lasted the longest got him all to themselves for the night, so he made a few bucks from the ring of spectators while he got laid too. I'd heard more than one conversation about his prowess in the sack—he had a huge dick and apparently knew how to use it.

Feeling much older than my thirty-one years, I stuck my fingers in my mouth and let out a shrill whistle that reached well above the noise from the hollering group. Heads swiveled in my direction, including the pair on the table. It was comical enough that I had to try not to laugh, but the headache was still sitting behind my eyes, making me irritable. With only Bronco and Dodo left of the officers, the others having already gone home, and the way they were all winding up, it wouldn't do to leave them unattended. Especially seeing as how one of my officers was the instigator and the other was his wingman, I didn't count them as able, or more like *willing*, to keep it from getting out of hand. A full-blown orgy in the bar would require extensive clean-up, and they all had their own rooms. They could take it elsewhere.

"Come on, guys, pack it up and move it somewhere private. And *not* the back rooms." My order was met with a few grumbles, but Bronco just winked at me with a grin while Dodo gave me a two-fingered salute then stuck them in the chick on top to hurry her along.

"Sorry, boss, give me two minutes," Bronco said as he assisted the other woman. Either she was already at the tipping point, or he really was that good because she came with a pissed off shout and slapped the other woman's ass. "Done! Tanya wins!"

Not-Tanya threw a glare at Bronco, but soon enough, she was changing her tune as the man that had been skirting around an outright proposition ten minutes ago picked her up and threw her over his shoulder.

"Night, Sevey," he offered as they went past, heading for the stairs as the rest of the crowd broke up to head off or find a room. Apparently, a piece of ass was a piece of ass, so I wasn't quite as irritated with him as I had been. I was still annoyed, and I planned to talk to him later about the attitude, but maybe I had been a bit testy over his invitation.

"Night, guys, I'll see you in the morning. We

have a job, so don't stay up too late." From the knowing look in Bronco's gaze, he knew exactly what I was referring to and gave me a quick dip of his head before taking off with Tanya. I made a mental note to ask if the women were going to be hanging around much, and if so, to have them vetted.

I flipped a switch under the bar top, shutting off the neon signs, before crossing the bar to lock the main doors. As I set the deadbolt, the unmistakable rumble of bike engines sounded in the distance, gaining volume as they approached.

As far as I was aware, everyone had dispersed for the night, and unless there was an emergency, I planned to send whoever it was on their way. Pulling one side of the double doors open, I peered out into the night, waiting for the riders to pull up.

A trio of black and chrome choppers stopped at the edge of the covered patio while a truck towing a trailer with a fourth bike parked a ways off to the side. As they killed the engines and shut the headlights off, the first pulled his helmet off.

Shock rocked my body as a ghost appeared in front of me. Except the dark features were on a full flesh-and-blood man who didn't appear to have changed a bit. I could only stare, my words lost in the million emotions flying through me.

The slamming of a door barely registered, but

the crunch of boots on the gravel, followed by a voice I never thought I'd hear again nearly had my legs buckling. Only the death grip I had on the door kept me upright.

"Well, Gus, I think she remembers us just fine," Lochlan said with a hint of mischief in his voice, but his gaze was inexplicably hard when it connected with mine.

Chapter Four

"You're dead," I managed, just above a whisper. Then the anger edged in, lending strength to my voice. "He said you were MIA, presumed dead, and we confirmed it with the mother chapter." *Did they think they could fuck off for* years, *leaving me alone with their kid, and I'd welcome them back when they let me think they'd* died?

"Obviously not," Loch shot back. "We're not the ones that changed our number and couldn't bother to wait like we promised." He conveniently left out anything to do with my last messages...or, ya know, the fact that there was a *baby*. *Unless they don't know.* I didn't understand how that could be possible, but I didn't deserve to be treated like *I* was the one in the wrong here.

Bewildered, pissed, and hurt, I glanced at Gus to find his face carefully blank. I had no idea what the fuck was going on, but I was starting to believe they had a vastly different understanding of events than I did. To top it off, the other two had removed their helmets and were watching us with avid interest. One of them, I recognized. He'd been the man Gus ran off that night at the bar.

Trying to figure out what they'd be doing at my bar if they weren't there for me or Opal, I went into protection mode. "Why are you here?" I also couldn't resist asking, "And why did you let everyone think you were dead?" I needed closure on that, at least, not to mention I had to figure out how to break the news that one of them was a father when all I really wanted to do was kick their asses, friends watching or not.

The guy from the bar spoke up before anyone else did. "We're retired and doing some traveling. Figured playing courier as we decide where we want to settle would earn some cash on the side and let us get to know our options a bit better. Ther—"

"Coot, you don't owe her an explanation. Let Boudreaux handle it," their dangerous-looking fourth barked out. Coot shut up, but he didn't seem too happy about it. There was sympathy in his eyes when he looked at me, though I didn't know what he thought he was feeling sorry about, but maybe he knew something I didn't yet.

The new man didn't even have helmet head. His blond hair was so sharply faded from the short length on top. It suited his stony countenance, an attractive one at that, but I chose to ignore him, turning to Gus to ask my question again since no one had bothered to answer it.

"Care to explain how you're here? And whatever you all have to deliver, just go ahead and get it so you can be on your way." I made the snap decision to talk to them about Opal *after* they left. They didn't get to waltz in after playing dead for the entirety of her short life without ever acknowledging she existed. We'd set up a parenting plan that we could agree on, or I'd leave it up to the courts to decide. My earlier decree that we go legit, or mostly anyhow, felt serendipitous now.

If only I could squash my feelings into a manageable compartment like everything else. The attraction was still well and alive, on my side anyway, along with that ache in my heart I'd felt when they had to leave that morning. Though it wasn't as bad as the day I'd found out about their supposed death. That had been debilitating.

"Loch, why don't you grab the box while I have a word with our hostess." It wasn't a suggestion so much as an order, and Lochlan retraced his steps. A few moments later, the tona cover popped up on the long bed of the truck.

But I'd caught on to the last word from Gus, and I wasn't too amused. It wasn't *required* to offer hospitality for other club members. It was considered a courtesy, one I hadn't planned on extending due to the situation. "Hostess? Did you call ahead to make sure we had availability? I don't recall seeing your group on the roster, but there's a decent enough hotel in town. You just follow the main road in and hang a left at the—"

Laughter cut me off, and I glared at the loudmouth, the one I hadn't even been introduced to yet. "I'm not sure what you find so amusing, but you can show some respect or get the fuck off my property," I snapped at him, letting all my frustration out on his rude ass.

"You're a little spitfire, aren't you, Prez? I apologize for being a poor...guest." His brows briefly raised with the 'guest' bit. His insincere tone and disdainful expression showed me exactly what he thought of me despite his words.

"Alright, Preppy, that's enough from the peanut gallery. I don't know you, nor do I care to. If you all have business, let's get it done. I'm ready to head home for the night, and you'll want to check in at the hotel before it gets much later, or you'll be sleeping in that fancy truck of yours. For the most part, Charity Falls closes down after ten o'clock, and there aren't too many options for lodging unless you keep on down the highway 'til you get to the city. Not sure which direction you boys came from, but it's about the same distance either way to get to a bigger bit of civilization. Just watch for the deer; they're a bitch to see in the dark." I ignored that the man had tried to insinuate himself, I wasn't raising to his bait, but his ears sure turned red when I called him Preppy. It would be the only way I'd refer to the asshole if I ever had the displeasure of running into him again.

"Wait, Sevey, seriously, we've been on the road all day, and we were assured each chapter we're scheduled to stop at has arrangements to put us up at their clubhouse. You know damn well the local hotels are full-up for opening day of hunting season —we already checked. We weren't going to bring it up because we didn't want to impose or cause any more bad blood than there already is, but we kept our word to do the delivery. Maybe you can keep yours too...for once." Gus had started out all reasonable and shit, but of course the discord between us shone through.

He was completely right that the couriers—members coming through from the mother chapter, usually trusted groups of nomads—always stayed when they brought a shipment in. I couldn't rightly throw them out on their ear and have it get around that my chapter wasn't hospitable. If they *were* here on official business, which I wasn't doubting at that point, I was fucked, and not in the fun way. Not that I'd had any of that since him and his cousin knocked my ass up. I'd debated on breaking that dry spell with the sheriff, but considering our past, that was a sketchy decision to make on another day. The four men hanging out in my parking lot needed to be dealt with and long gone before I made any plans to get up to the horizontal tango.

With a long-suffering sigh, I unlatched the second door and propped both open, gesturing for them to get on with it. "C'mon, grab your shit and my shipment and get in here. I'm ready to lock up and head home. I'll show you how to use the other entrance and get you some keys." The mention of the main clubhouse entrance through the back had me yanking my phone out to text my aunt. I needed her to get Opal out of there before I took them up.

Me: I have a group I need to put up for the night, but I want Opal home before I bring them up. I'll keep them in the chapel until you're on your way.

Shit, that sounds ominous.

Me: Nothing dangerous, so don't worry. I'll explain when I get home.

RagBag: I checked the monitors when I heard them come in, Severine.

I groaned at the full name and knew she had recognized them—it'd be hard not to with the pics I'd kept. Which was why they weren't going near my office.

Me: I'm not hiding her, but something doesn't add up, and they're being more than prickly. I don't want Opal in the middle of it. We'll sort it later. Just get her home, please.

RagBag: I'll take the little miss while you handle those boys. Don't do anything we'll have to clean up and bury. I'm not sure that sheriff friend of yours would be able to cover your ass, and Opal needs her mama.

RagBag: Also, let me know if I need to get the shovels out...

I couldn't help but smile at Aunt Flo's message. That woman always had, and always would, have my back, no matter what I got myself into.

"Would you mind waiting to flirt until we've

handled our business?" Lochlan griped as he lugged a whole-ass footlocker past me and into the chapel, his snide glance at my phone a clue as to what had prompted his uncalled-for comment.

"I believe that the rules of hospitality extend to the *guests*, Lochlan. Try not to be a dick, yeah? And while you're at it—mind your own damn business."

I politely didn't mention that he was an idiot for not waiting on me to get the handcart from the storeroom so he didn't have to pack the trunk. Though I couldn't deny the way the muscles of his arms and back flexed was eye candy or that I was forcing myself not to glance lower to check out his ass.

Crossing my fingers, I sent up a prayer to whatever god or goddess oversaw getting down with Mr. Buzz-Buzz that Opal would stay asleep while I relieved myself of the effects of my overactive panty hamster.

There was no way I could deal with them without emptying the tank, so to speak. And I definitely was *not* thinking that pair of earplugs would take care of eliminating whatever nonsense came out of their mouths if I decided I could put my mad aside and take one for a quick spin...for old time's sake, of course, not because I was hoping some sparkly fairy would drop down and poof my life into a fairytale where the rough-and-tumble princes worshiped their woman for the rest of her days and polished her, uh, chrome on the regular.

I must have zoned out because a loud snort from directly behind me nearly scared me out of my skin... and I might have pissed myself a little. Ya know, mommy bladder and all that shiznit. Craning my head over my shoulder to find Coot, I ignored the heat blooming in my cheeks at his knowing glance flicking from me to where Lochlan had disappeared. Not that I could miss his low voice, almost a whisper.

"It's still your dry season around here. Better be careful with that heat between you two. Wouldn't want to start a fire, now would you?" He was so close, the husky rumble reverberated in my ear, snapping me out of my surprise to jolt sideways and away from him, banging my hip on one of the tables hard enough to rattle the chairs on it.

"No worries there, bud. I hear there's a good chance of frost hitting soon." Not the most eloquent comeback, but I strode off just the same as if it had been a zinger and went outside to see what the hold-up was with the other two.

They were just heading in, with two heavy-looking duffel bags slung over each shoulder.

"Am I good to lock up now? I'll give you keys to go out the back, and there's parking back there too if you'd rather. I don't like chancing the bar being left unlocked when it's not open, so it's only the back entrance unless there's an emergency." I realized I was overexplaining even though I didn't owe them anything of the sort and snapped my mouth shut. Preppy smirked at me, but he wisely kept whatever he was thinking to himself.

"We're good. We'll be on our way in the morning." Gus' answer was clipped and his countenance hard.

If that was how he wanted it, it was fine by me. I'd just ignore the contrary pain my chest twinged with. It was what I wanted, what I *needed*, but my emotions weren't quite on board yet. They were still reeling from the surreality of them being alive, right along with the rest of me. Or at least most of the rest of me. My libido was being a little tart, waving the open sign like a fifties flag girl at a street race.

As we got into the chapel, they set their bags down, and I turned just in time to catch them canvasing the room, scanning it from one end to the other, before they relaxed. I hadn't the foggiest on what, or who, they had expected to be in here, but they were definitely on high alert. I chose not to comment on it, going to where the footlocker was sitting on the large table with Lochlan and Coot guarding it.

"Surprised your old man lets you hang out

around here by yourself with strange men," Preppy quipped behind me.

Doing my best not to rise to the bait, I put my back against the table and held my hand out before asking, "Who has the key?"

"What key?" Lochlan retorted, confusion on his face.

"The paper. You should have a key that matches the files... Fuck." Dread filled my bones as my gaze darted from one to the other until I'd made a full round back to Lochlan.

Jesus fucking Christ, what if they're undercover to bust me? I hadn't even questioned it. Being who they were, I just assumed, but they were also military... My thoughts spiraled from there. I freaked out internally while trying to keep my shit together on the outside. Other than my minor slip, which could have just as easily been an insult, I could backtrack and get them out of here, call the crew in, and sanitize the place before morning.

My plans to clean house in a hurry were interrupted by Gus. "Oh, I thought you meant a key key. They said you'd have a copy to get the footlocker open and made it clear we weren't getting one. I have the inventory key right here." He held out a large index card, but I was afraid to take it, leaving him hanging while I yanked my phone from my pocket, sending a message to my aunt in an instant.

The return message I got back had relief surging through me so fast I felt like a balloon that had just had all its air let out. She'd already vetted their arrival and had been about to message me. God, I loved that woman.

Some of what I'd tried to hide must not have gone unnoticed because Lochlan took immediate offense. "We're not narcs, Sevey. No matter our personal feelings about you, we're loyal to the Club."

I held my head high, refusing to quail under the comment. "Yes, I just got confirmation, something I should have done before I let you in. Frankly, my head is a bit all over the place after seeing you're alive when we were assured you were not almost three years ago. I can't be too careful. I have people that depend on me, and my club members have lives I shouldn't be taking chances with." I took the card from Gus and turned my back on all of them while I fished for the right key on the ring. I was just slipping the lock off when Lochlan couldn't hold his tongue any longer, though the comment wasn't directed at me, but to one of the others.

"She's not even wearing a ring, can't be too serious. Unless she was already involved back then and just doesn't wear one at all so she can make promises she doesn't plan to keep."

At that point, I well and truly lost my shit. "God-damnit!" I yelled, slapping the table with my hand, the smack like a crackshot in the abrupt silence. "We spent one night together. One! I can't help that you—You know what? It's not worth rehashing." Taking a breath to calm myself then blowing it out to help release the stress of it all, I opened my eyes and focused on them. "Let's get the inventory done quickly, so I can message my contact that it's all here, then I'll show you to your rooms and give you a quick tour so you can eat and get your beauty sleep." I'd never admit road rough looked good on any of them, even if I were being tortured, but if they were going to pick at me, I could do the same to them. Rules of hospitality be damned.

Gus shot a pleading glance at Lochlan while Preppy told him to shut it. I guessed he was done fucking around as well.

I started pulling files from the footlocker, matching them to the key and verifying all the pages were there before going for the supplies I'd been sorely in need of. The special inks, dyes, and other supplies to forge solid documentation for a myriad of states wasn't something I could waltz into the nearest office supply store to procure.

Remembering that I'd need to do a set in the morning, I set enough aside to lock in my desk while everything else went back into the footlocker to get stored in one of the safe rooms I used to practice my trade.

With a quick "Be right back," I took what I had set aside to my office before I lugged the rest with us. I fully didn't expect to be followed. It was my damn clubhouse and bar after all, and in theory, they should have kept their asses in the chapel. It only took me a few seconds to pop the supplies in a drawer and lock it, but that was enough time for a low whistle to ring out behind me.

"No wonder you got your panties all up in a twist when we showed up." And then louder, Preppy yelled for the cousins. "Boudreaux! Get your asses in here. I think there's a hell of a lot of explaining that needs to be done."

I felt myself pale for the second time that night. "Get the fuck out of my clubhouse." My voice was low and deadly as I snatched the picture that sat on my desk out of his hand. It held a picture of my daughter and both of the guys, and it wasn't any of his fucking business.

The dick didn't move, and before I could escalate matters, the other three popped in and froze, staring warily between me and the interloper. Gus, either stupid or brave, or maybe both, edged in between us, his back to me as he confronted his friend.

"What's happened, Ares?" His voice held a hint of accusation, and I had to wonder how well they knew this man and why they'd let him follow me.

Holding his hands up, Ares, a name that fit him well enough with his dangerous demeanor, tipped a finger down to point behind Gus. "Think you might want to turn around and take a peek at what your lady friend is holding."

Gus turned halfway around to give me a questioning glance, but Lochlan's stare felt like it was boring a hole through me, and I caved, looking up at him.

Nervousness flashed across his face as he asked, in a gentler tone than he'd used since they showed up, "Sevey, what's he talking about?"

Closing my eyes for a brief second, I opened them again as I flipped the frame over. The only sound in the room was the sharp inhalations from the cousins and a whispered "Oh, shit," from Coot. There was no mistaking she belonged to Gus or Lochlan, especially not with their pictures side by side.

Chapter Five

"Were you going to tell us?" Lochlan asked, a hint of accusation in his tone.

I swallowed hard, tamped down the urge to lash out at him, and nodded before setting the frame back on the desk. Their eyes tracked it like magnets, but they didn't try to come forward to pick it up. "I'd like to finish what we were doing, then you can explain where you've been and why you let me think you were dead." My voice was calm, something I was mighty proud of at that moment, as I pointedly glanced at the doorway with raised brows.

They got the hint, and at Coot's urging, three of them filed out. Preppy, not Ares, because I wasn't fucking changing his name, must have realized he'd massively misjudged me as his eyes were full of apology. He gave me a short nod before he left my office to follow the others.

After locking up, turning all but the security lights out, and solidifying my composure, I returned to the chapel with the handcart in tow. I didn't bother to ask for help, I didn't need it, but Preppy stepped up, moving the footlocker to stand on its end and securing it with the strap.

"If you don't mind leading the way, I'll get it where it's going," he offered, earning a double-take from me and glares from the other three.

Not caring who the hell moved it, I headed down the hall to the back entrance of the kitchen and on into the walk-in refrigerator. At the back wall, there was a second door to the freezer, but next to it, another was hidden, disguised as just another silver, insulated panel. Popping open the lid to the thermostat, I entered my code to the safe room, causing the panel to unlatch.

"Are you sure you want to be showing us this?" Coot asked, staring wide-eyed at the set-up.

With a roll of my own, I pointed out the obvious. "You already know what's in here. Besides, you're not narcs, remember?" That, and they wouldn't know the code were they to try to get in without me. I'd be changing it tomorrow after the sheriff made his visit... I always did.

"Suit yourself," he said with a shrug, craning his neck to see around me and Preppy as I helped him guide the footlocker through the door.

Gus and Lochlan stayed outside, but I could vaguely hear them talking in low voices. I assumed they were discussing Opal and getting their story straight. I hoped it was a good one after everything.

Knowing it was time to have that discussion, I locked up and set off to give them a short tour and get one of the extra keys so I could leave as soon as we'd all had our say. I just wasn't sure if the other two were gonna stick around to witness it all or if we'd have some privacy. Didn't particularly care either way.

"You really expect me to believe that shit?" I asked incredulously, struggling to keep from raising my voice. Some of the rooms were occupied by the group from earlier, and while they were decently insulated, they weren't soundproof.

Frustration fairly oozed from Gus as he ran a hand through his short hair for at least the third time since we'd shut ourselves up in one of the double rooms, but it was Lochlan that barked back at me.

"It's the fucking *truth*, so yes, I expect you to believe it. It took us three weeks to make contact with our superiors and get a ride back to civilization *after* we completed our job. And no, we can't verify where we were or what we were doing because it's classified. Even if we told you, there's not any documentation to prove it!"

"Fine, I can accept that part of it, but when you got back stateside, why didn't you answer my messages? It was pretty damn clear that I needed you to get in touch and that I was pregnant. For fuck's sake, I went into premature labor after your buddy told me you were gone." I couldn't keep the hurt and betrayal out of my voice.

"We're so sorry, Sevey. Whether we worked out or not, we never would have skipped out on you being pregnant," Gus interjected, but I wasn't quite ready to get on to that portion of the explanation. I just stared at them both until Lochlan looked to Preppy.

Chapter Six

Nerves ate at my stomach as I walked the sheriff out. The guys were not so unobtrusively hanging out in the clubhouse, waiting to meet Opal, and I regretted not asking them to stay upstairs until I was done with my meeting. Their eyes tracking my every move had me jumpy as hell, and it was setting off the sheriff's radar.

"You taking on new members?" he asked as he stopped short, blocking the door. We both knew he was fishing for who they were and what they were doing here. If I didn't fess up now, he'd only poke around until he got enough information to run a background check on them. Embarrassing as he could be when his curiosity and suspicions were piqued, he was an unofficial asset to the club and a friend as well.

"Josh, don't you dare start. I have it handled," I warned in a low voice that wouldn't carry. Just because I knew he'd keep on didn't mean I wouldn't try to send him off for the time being. He grinned big enough to show his dimple, but the challenge in his eyes had me rolling mine and spilling enough to get him off my case before he got on it. "You remember when I had Opal?" He nodded, expression instantly hardening. "Well, the two that look alike? One of them is her father. They're not so dead after all. There was some sort of mix-up, then crossed wires, and last night they showed up to deliver my shipment."

He wasn't quick enough to hide the reaction I'd expected, but he *was* quick to cover it up. I knew he'd been biding his time, dropping hints here and there that he was interested in getting back together even though it had been more than a decade since we'd dated. I was grateful that he pushed that topic to the side when he finally responded. "I thought they looked an awful lot like the photos you have in your office, but I figured it was coincidence since they're supposed to be dead and all." The last was said with a hint of bitterness, and I had to wonder if this was going to be a problem. I trusted him and wouldn't entertain the thought that he'd turn on me. He'd destroy his own life, as well as the innocents we worked to protect, if he attempted it, but he could make himself a thorn in my side if he really wanted to.

Running my fingers through my dark hair while releasing a breath, I shrugged and offered what I didn't mind sharing. "I'm sure it will all come out eventually, but right now, it's more than a little awkward, and I'd rather keep it private until we've sorted out how we're going to go about them being in Opal's life."

"Them? And *just* Opal's, or yours too?" Of course he'd caught on to the first part. I knew it was bound to be a hot topic.

"They don't care who the biological father is. Plans are currently in the beginning stages since they haven't even met her yet, but they'd both like to fill the role. They have this whole thing about sharing, and that was part of their life plan..." I trailed off as Josh's eyebrows climbed until I thought they'd raise plumb off his face if they got much higher. "Maybe that was a bit of TMI. Sorry about that."

"You had a threesome with them?" he asked loudly enough for me to hush him.

"Yes!" I hissed back. "Now lower your voice before everyone knows my damn business."

"I thought you'd just— Never mind, that's not important, I suppose. Are you sure you don't want me to stick around? Are you comfortable with them being here?" His concern was palpable, yet the ulterior motive lurking just behind it had my head shaking in response before he'd quite finished.

"Nah, I'm good, but I'll give you a call if that changes. Your package will be ready for you late tonight, and I'll have Tee run it by if that works for you."

He hesitated, and I thought he'd insist on picking up the documents himself, but then he seemed to think better of it, nodding before slipping his sunglasses on and heading out.

I stood there, staring at the closed door, while I prepared myself for my daughter to meet her other parents. It was a surreal moment, one I'd never thought would happen, and despite the misgivings I might have about them in general, I was strangely content that they wanted to be there to watch Opal grow up.

"I can't get over how well she talks. I can actually understand most of what she's saying," Gus marveled at our toddler, who was holding court in her bedroom. She'd introduced just about all of her dolls and stuffed animals to Lochlan, and the man was just as enthralled as his cousin. The feeling was mutual from Opal, though I wasn't sure that she completely understood that they were her dads yet.

"She still has quite a bit of baby jabber going on, and I imagine that'll last another year or so, but without too many kids her age to hang out with, she's mostly been around adults, so she's picked up a lot of words since she started talking." I wouldn't mention the profanities she'd also adopted. So far, she'd been a good little darling, but I knew it was only a matter of time until she popped off with an F-bomb.

Lochlan spoke up, letting on that he'd been paying attention to both of us as well as Opal. "You've done great with her, Sevey. I can't decide if she looks more like you or us. She's changed some since the photo where she was looking like a mini Boudreaux."

Emotion squeezed at my chest as my eyes met his. He seemed just as affected given the vulnerable expression he sported. "Kids grow and change quickly, especially when they're younger. Opal turned two back at the beginning of summer; that picture was from her birthday." I didn't address the compliment, uncomfortable with the praise since I hadn't raised her alone. Aunt Flo helped tremendously with the day-to-day care, and even the crew stepped in when I had business that couldn't wait.

Gus' attention turned from where Opal was now picking at her snacks on her tea table to me at the mention of her birthday. Confusion wrinkled the space between his brows as he asked, "When was she born?"

With the anxiety that still creeped up on me every now and then when I remembered how Opal had arrived in the world, more prominent today with the shock of their arrival, I missed the undercurrent of accusation in his voice. "June tenth."

"We shipped out the first week of October," Lochlan said flatly. Glancing between the two of them, I found disappointment and anger mirrored from one to the other.

It dawned on me that they were getting at the dates not adding up, and I had to bite my tongue to avoid laying into them. Opal, sensing the change in the atmosphere, abandoned her snack sorting to climb on her bed and get behind my back, further pissing me off. Trying to play it off, I shot a glare at both men then stood up before scooping my little miss into my arms.

"Do you want Aunt Flo, or do you want to play in here? I have some work I need to do, but I'll be back by dinner time, and we can have a game night." The promise of games, particularly the dancing video game, perked her right up, and I even got a grin as she told me she wanted our aunt. Packing her off downstairs with me, I handed her off to Aunt Flo at the bottom. She was all smiles for Opal, but coolly aloof with Lochlan and Gus. She might not know what had happened, but she was an intuitive woman. "I won't be too long. Text if you want me to order something in for dinner." She nodded and headed back up the stairs with Opal after the guys moved out of her way. As soon as they disappeared past the landing, I stabbed a finger toward the front door. "Get the fuck out of my house."

"Are you seriously pissed at us? We have the right to know if she's not ours." That time, Lochlan was conscientious about Opal being in the house, yet even though he kept his voice low, there was still a deal of venom in his tone.

"Sure you do, and I would have told you last night if she wasn't, but you don't bring shit like that up in front of her!" I hissed back at him. "Did you miss the part where I told you I had her early because I was so upset you were *dead*?"

Gus blanched when he realized how badly he'd stepped in it by questioning Opal's date of birth. "You didn't elaborate, so I assumed they stopped it." He looked at Lochlan whose face was stony, but I was starting to get that that was a default for him. The fun-loving guy from the rally wasn't the norm when there were even semi-serious matters at hand.

He shrugged instead of offering the apology I'd expected. "I didn't think to ask how early she was. Like Gus, I figured you'd have said if there was something we needed to know."

I hadn't realized I'd been holding on to a tiny bit of hope that we could maybe be a family until it dissolved in the face of their recalcitrance. "Opal was a couple weeks earlier than the safety window, but thankfully, she didn't have any complications from it. She's healthy, happy, and I'll make damned sure she stays that way—so don't fuck with me."

The short drive across the property to the clubhouse was a silent one, and when Coot asked what was wrong, as none of us had pleasant faces, I just shook my head and walked away. While finishing up the admin work Aunt Flo had passed on to me for the bar, all four of my guests showed up. They had a few more stops to make for deliveries, but Lochlan and Gus wanted to stay while Coot and Preppy finished up, and the latter also wanted to return. Permanently. I couldn't fathom how the cousins and I would get on after the last twenty-four hours, but I didn't have it in me to deny them a full-time relationship with Opal. And apparently where they went, so did the other two.

Chapter Seven

Six Weeks Later

"What do I have to do to get you to stop calling me Preppy?" The man in question was looking, and sounding, seriously put out about the nickname. All four of my new residents had taken to popping up here and there with offers to help out. Offers I begrudgingly accepted even though my crew members should already be doing the jobs. Apparently, there was a lack of competence going on in my club, something I'd be addressing in church real fucking soon.

"I'm not calling you Ares. God of War, my stretch-marked ass." The last was more to myself, mumbled under my breath, but the room was small and quiet, so he definitely heard me.

At his glower, I shrugged and kept on with the inventory tally. One of the bartenders thought we'd been having to order a bit too often, so I was taking a day to go through the storage room before comparing it to the receipts to see what was what. If someone from my crew was getting sticky fingers, they were liable to lose the whole hand. "Can you reach those boxes up there behind you? I need to check what's in them and how many. I've already found boxes that should have been compiled and broken down—like it's fucking hard to move one set of bottles that match the other into the same box. Someone is going to be missing a strip of hide when I get through with them."

"I'll be happy to help with that if you'd like. We don't have enough to do hanging around here. Not that we mind hanging around," he said in his defense, holding his hands up when he got glared at. "Just meaning feel free to put us to work. We'd be happy to pitch in, and we're used to keeping shit organized. We'll eventually have to find jobs, but we've got enough stashed back to keep us for a while yet."

Vacillating between saying what I was feeling or zipping my lips, I went through two more boxes before turning to face him. Hoping I wasn't making a mistake, I revealed my concerns. "It's my club, my problem. Yes, you're technically full members, but I feel that it looks like I can't handle my shit if I let you come in and help straighten out what shouldn't be fucked up in the first place. And if you share any of this, I'm booting your ass out, but some of my decisions have caused friction that I didn't anticipate. A few crew members aren't into the changes that are happening, and it's getting to the point that they're going to be formally reprimanded. I'm afraid I'm going to lose members. We've only been an official chapter for three years, and I've managed to fuck it all up." I finally fell silent after getting my worries off my chest. The person I chose to vent to could have been better, and maybe it would come back to bite me in the ass, but despite the way he rubbed me wrong, I didn't get the vibe that he was disingenuous or unreliable.

He looked just as surprised at first, but then something I couldn't quite put my finger on crept into his gaze. I had an inkling that I'd just gotten myself a new BFF for lack of a better term.

"Jesse," he blurted out, crossing his arms over his chest and flaring his nose in challenge.

"What?" I was lost as to what he meant, but it was obvious he'd come to some sort of decision.

"You don't want to call me Ares, so call me Jesse. That's my name, Jesse O'Brien." The offer of a compromise was a tipping point for us, one I was fine with.

"I suppose I can retire Preppy then. Jesse sorta suits you anyhow." After agreeing to his suggestion, I got a half smile, something that made him go from dark and dangerous to still dangerous, but more in the melt-your-panties way.

"Deal. Now, competition is always a good way to get your people in order. If they think they might lose their position, they tend to step it up. Or, you know, they may need to be culled for the better of the group. So tell me how I can help, and I'll get on it with the guys."

I thought about it for a minute while I continued to work. After gathering my thoughts, I asked what was probably a stupid question, but again, my intuition told me Jesse wouldn't lie to me. "Can I trust you? Like, *really* trust you, without you running off to your friends to fill them in?"

His answer wasn't instant; he took a second, but he seemed genuine when he spoke. "I'm not in the habit of keeping secrets from them. We've been a unit and friends for too long for that. But..." He forestalled me when I went to tell him to forget it. "If it doesn't endanger or betray any of them, whatever you share with me will stay between us."

It wasn't perfect, but if he'd said yes without the caveat, I might not have believed him. Did that make me fickle? Maybe. But I felt much better knowing he had a code that he'd stick to. Though I did wonder what the friend and unit speak was about since usually, in my experience, military men referred to each other as brothers.

"Well, remember you asked for it when the to-do list is longer than you are tall." The warning was clue enough that we'd reached an accord. Then I set about outlining what I hoped to get done before winter set in, as well as the tasks that appeared to be being neglected.

~

Between the meeting where I royally chewed ass and the assistance from the guys, the next week was a productive one. My VP was pissed, but he'd been off for months, and I wasn't quite sure how to fix whatever was wrong. He claimed it was growing pains from our transition into legal business and the uncertainty of what we'd do if the laws changed again that worried him, but it felt like more than that. I figured I'd give him some space and see if he sorted himself out before I intervened, though it bugged me to do so.

On the bright side, Opal had all but attached herself to her dads. She'd even started calling them that. The others were Uncle Jesse and Uncle Levi. When I found out *why* he was called Coot, I wasn't having my daughter use it and had demanded he choose something else. I could still hear Gus snickering as he informed me that there wasn't a pair of panties Levi hadn't been able to drop yet, hence Coot, which was shortened from Cooter. When I mentioned I'd turned him down, he said that didn't count since he hadn't actually gotten a chance thanks to Gus and Lochlan heading him off. At that point, the conversation had taken a turn into uncomfortable territory as it was blatant he'd be interested in giving it a go, and the cousins didn't seem to mind at all. Wondering if the ship had sailed on *their* interest, or whether they just didn't mind sharing all around, I'd hightailed it out of there, not ready to find out either way.

I should have known I couldn't avoid the topic forever though, and the two new club whores had just shown me that their interest had indeed moved on. With the bar closed to the public for the night, it was club members only, a chance to let loose since everyone had been working hard to get my plans under way.

I'd kept half an eye on the new women, as I usually did any new member, prospect, or hanger-on, and now I sort of wished I had gone home early and left the festivities to Tee or Tank. My sergeant-at-arms, a crazy fucker that looked like a red-headed Viking who didn't take shit from anybody, Tank probably would have been the better choice, but he had an elderly mother at home that he didn't like to leave alone at night. I couldn't blame him. I had Opal waiting on me as well, but I had the benefit of a much shorter drive. I could walk if I decided to drink, whereas Tank would have to tag in one of the prospects if he needed a DD.

It was too late to delegate, with Tank already being gone and Tee partying it up, so I stayed behind the bar, stocking it while Coot and Jesse forwent the party to install the electronic locks on all of the storerooms. They'd just arrived earlier in the afternoon, and the guys had wanted to get the job done. The new locks had user-specific codes, were hooked up to the wi-fi, and the entry log would automatically get emailed to me each day. It was an easy solution to an irritating problem.

We had indeed been short miscellaneous bottles of alcohol, enough to fill several cases when it came down to it. Spills, overpouring, and even accidental breaking wouldn't account for what was missing. I hadn't been able to narrow down the person, or persons, responsible, but my crew had gotten a warning that we didn't help ourselves to bar or club property without either me or Tee authorizing it, and he swore he hadn't given it. No one said differently, so I took him at his word and prepared myself to clean house when I found out who was fucking around in shit they shouldn't be.

As I polished the bar to within an inch of its life, avoiding the show Nancy and Tanya were putting on for Gus and Lochlan, I wished the thief would magically pop up so I could beat the shit out of someone. It wasn't the women's fault that I was still hung up on two men that were free to do what they wanted, but all the same, I had the urge to stake my nonexistent claim and kick their half-naked asses out of my bar.

Fully aware I shouldn't do that just because I was jealous, I signaled one of the prospects to man the bar so I could take a break and regain my composure. It was a damn good thing I did as at that moment, Tanya decided to press her suit and straddled Lochlan, flashing me and everyone else her unpantied crotch. I didn't wait around to see what happened next, zipping down the hall to hide in the first room I came to. Keying in my code, I was inside and had my back against the closed door before I realized the room was occupied.

I wasn't sure who was more shocked, me or Jesse and Coot, but they recovered a hell of a lot faster than I did. Pulling his lips from around Jesse's impressively thick dick, Coot raised a brow and, using the hand gripping the base of said dick, tilted it in my direction. "Wanna lick, little lady?" he asked, all polite and shit like he was offering me a Blow-Pop.

I blinked at the man on his knees before my eyes traveled up to lock on Jesse's heated ones. Sex, public or private, was common enough around the clubhouse and didn't faze me in the least, but something about finding the two of them together drew me like a magnet. It had me ready to abandon my dry spell while also presenting me with the dual purpose of soothing my hurt pride and bruised heart.

"If you'd prefer I get on my knees alongside Coot for you to take my place, that can be arranged. Or I can put my dick away, and you can sit down and tell us what you're running from. I'm assuming it's Boudreaux?" His intuition was spot on, but I couldn't use them that way without giving them a heads up. Upset as I was about the situation, I wouldn't wreck their friendship, not that I was brave enough to take them up on their offer.

"They're with the new girls, and I couldn't stand to watch it. I'll let you two finish up here. I'm just gonna go." My hand gripped the handle even though leaving was the last thing I wanted to do, both for curiosity's sake and in hopes of driving intrusive thoughts of the bar scene from my head.

"Stupid fuckers,"" Coot muttered as he gracefully stood up and stepped toward me. He didn't stop until he was close enough to thread an arm between me and the door, only leaving an inch of space between us. Breath feathering against my lips from his as he tipped my chin up with his free hand, Coot scrambled my brain further. "The way I see it, you have three options. Go home and leave the bar to me and Ares, go back out there and get shit faced while we keep you company, or you can let us make you forget about your problems for a bit and then decide what you want to do."

"I don't want to cause problems," I whispered, feeling my will to leave desert me.

His fingers released my chin to trail across my jaw and around to the nape of my neck until they threaded through my hair, where they settled, cradling the back of my head and anchoring me in place. "You let us worry about any fallout, not that I think there would be any if you choose to be with us. The four of us... We have an understanding, if you will. So what'll it be, Severine?"

A shiver coursed through me at his use of my name. His expression was dead set on mine, urging me to make a decision, though I didn't feel pressured in the least.

Throwing caution to the wind, tired of wishing I could have what others did, *act* like others did, I gave him my answer. "The third one."

"Good girl, Sevey," Jesse intoned, less than an arm's length from my side. Intent as I'd been on Coot, I hadn't seen the deadly man move. I nearly gulped with the nerves that wracked me when I met his stare and saw the intense intent written there. *What the hell did I just agree to?*

While I was busy trying to decide if I'd gotten myself in over my head, Coot closed the space between us, pressing his chest to mine and fusing lips, puffy from the blow job he'd been giving, to mine. That was all it took for the barrier I'd held firm to crumble. My pussy was already waving the white flag of surrender, opening the gates like it'd been under siege all this time or some shit.

Chapter Eight

As I softened under Coot's onslaught, he pulled me to him, spinning us until Jesse's broad chest was against my back—which stiffened as the latter's hands crept under the bottom of my shirt, landing on the loose skin of my stomach.

Breaking my lips away from the man in front of me, I tried to arch my back to escape Jesse's wandering hands, but there wasn't any space to do so. "I had a baby," I blurted out before slipping my hands beneath his, embarrassment rolling through me. The changes my body went through while carrying Opal had left very visible, very permanent marks behind that had played a part in my reluctance to resume any type of casual intimacy. A random hook-up already felt awkward enough despite that being my norm years ago. Add in body issues, and that just tanked the interest all to hell.

Coot reared back to stare down at me, concern and confusion in his eyes. "Uh, yes, we're aware. Unless you mean you had one recently that we don't know about?" His eyes instantly went to my stomach area like he'd be able to tell just from looking. If I wasn't so uncomfortable, I'd find it amusing, but I didn't want to have to explain that I was afraid they'd find me ugly, so I shook my head, trying to figure out a way to gracefully bow out of the imminent activities. Jesse, quickly figuring out what my issue was, twined his fingers with mine, refusing to let me move them away.

"I can for sure promise that I don't mind anything you're trying to hide under your clothes. Coot here won't either. If it'll make you feel better, we can give you a list of shit neither of us likes about our own appearances."

Understanding dawned on Coot's face, and an instant later, he'd dropped back down onto his knees, his head coming nearly to my chest. The two of them were uncannily in tune as Jesse tightened his fingers around mine and lifted his arms, taking mine with them until they rested near his shoulders on either side of my head. "You say the word, and I'll stop, but don't make the call because you think I'm judging you. Have Jesse fill you in on Sasquatch and Uniball while I get you a bit more comfortable for what we have planned."

Sasquatch? Uniball? When the fuck did they make plans *that involve* me? It was hard enough to catch my breath with Coot intent on getting me out of my clothes, and the stiff length pressing into my ass, let alone catch my damn chaotic thoughts. A millisecond before he lifted the hem of my shirt, I lost my courage and squeaked out, "Lights."

His gaze flicked from mine to Jesse behind me before he voiced his opinion on that. "It'll be pitch black in here, not to mention I'll be disappointed to miss seeing what I plan on eating."

Taking my fear and throwing it out the proverbial window, I let my eyes drift shut and jerked my head in agreement. It didn't lessen my nerves, but at least I wouldn't have to see any negative reaction he might have when my post-baby body was bared in all its imperfect glory.

"Relax, Sevey, we've got you," Jesse murmured in my ear, causing a shiver to work through me. Or maybe that was from Coot popping the button on my jeans. My breath hitched as he lowered the zipper and started to shimmy them down, underwear and all. As he paused to lift one foot, then the other, to get my boots off, Jesse filled me in on their cosmetic flaws. "You haven't seen me without a shirt on yet, though that'll happen soon enough if I have my way, but about the time I graduated high school, I started getting body hair." It was hard to concentrate on what he was saying with Coot about to get up close and personal with my long-neglected pussy, but I did my best to pay attention to them both. "After enlisting, I was dubbed Sasquatch in basic training. You see, thanks to genetics, I have a hairy back. And I don't mean a little bit. I have full-blown patches on both shoulder blades that nearly meet in the middle. It's not my favorite feature, and besides the scars we've picked up, a hazard of our profession, I also have a scar from having my appendix out. Suffice it to say, I doubt you'd have more than a bit of empathy for any of it, if you addressed it at all."

I blinked down at Coot, both to watch as he lifted one of my legs over his shoulder and to see if Jesse was telling the truth, though I didn't see the point in lying about something like that. He only gave me a wink before blowing a stream of air across my pussy, and while I was mid shiver at the sensation, he dove in, unerringly using his tongue to part my folds and latch onto my clit. There was no preamble or work-up, just balls to the wall suction and tongue action that had the leg I stood on nearly buckling. I didn't know why I thought he'd take a different approach, especially with the fact that we were in a storeroom in my bar that wasn't exactly conducive to more than a quickie, but I'd sort of expected that he'd have done more than get access to my bottom half and go to town on my box. It felt like something teens would do, fumbling in the dark, though there was a distinct lack of fumbling, and it sure as hell wasn't dark.

A dark chuckle came from Jesse at my squirming, but I couldn't help it. Coot was wrecking me with each flick of tongue and pull of his lips. I'd never gone from mildly horny to wet, clenching pussy so fast in my goddamn life.

Voice unsteady, I urged Jesse to continue his story, the last of my request getting strangled as Coot turned me loose long enough to wet two fingers in his mouth, barely pausing to check if I was ready before sliding them home. The stretch was immediate, my groan echoing his. "Fuck, darlin', you're making my dick jealous of my fingers with this hot-ass pussy."

Jesse's hands flexed on mine in response as he resumed speaking, huskier than he had been, as Coot returned to my clit and worked his fingers into that hook that would make my supporting leg fail for sure. I almost didn't catch a damn thing he said, but I didn't want to be rude when the man was trying to put me at ease. "Soon after that, I started having the shit waxed off, and now that we have more time for it, I'll probably see about getting laser removal."

"This has got to be the craziest hook-up ever, just so you know," I managed, nearing my peak from Coot's skillful touch.

"If I'm showing you my furry-ass back, this best be more than a casual hook-up." Jesse's disgruntled tone distracted me enough to stall my orgasm, and I was half-worried he'd call a stop to it all if I denied it wasn't only casual.

"I don't fuck random men in my supply closets on the regular if that helps any. Now, what's a uniball?"

Jesse's grunt didn't give me much faith that I'd reassured him at all, but he answered me anyway. "It's a who, not a what, and it's what Coot started getting called after an unofficial grappling tournament went wrong. The other guy accidentally came down right on Coot's balls. Had to have surgery and now only has one. Hence the 'Uniball' reference."

"Holy shit, ouch, dude." And also...I was kinda curious about the difference, but I wasn't about to mention that part as I stared down at the man between my legs. He shrugged like it didn't matter, which I highly doubted, but I was distracted from pursuing it when he doubled his efforts and rapidly pushed me off the cliff into a climax that left his cheeks embarrassingly shiny and wet. I was straight-up afraid to see the mess I'd made of his hand.

"It sucked at the time," he said, coming up for air as I tried to recover. Then he popped his fingers in his mouth. I couldn't decide if I was grossed out or grossly turned on by the sight. "But it all works like normal now that it's all healed up. I'll prove it here in just a minute as soon as I locate the condoms." He turned to rummage in their toolbag as I narrowed my eyes and turned my head to look up at Jesse.

"How the hell do you two have condoms in here already? That sure looks like you had the same plans as the other two, and I happened to conveniently show up." I sounded waspish to my own ears, but I didn't care. I still wanted an answer.

"I grabbed them in town when I was at the store earlier. It was *convenient* to throw them in since we went straight to installing the locks and haven't been upstairs yet," Coot said, briefly stopping his digging to roll his eyes at me while Jesse chuckled against my back. I felt a little silly, but it made me feel better to know they weren't screwing anything that walked.

"Does that brain of yours ever shut off for five

minutes?" Jesse demanded, putting enough space between us to lift my shirt off over my head. He spun me until I faced him, then took his own shirt off before he pulled me against his chest. "Just hush now. Let us make you feel good."

There was no time to be embarrassed about standing there in just my bra because Jesse took my lips with his and immediately demanded entry with this tongue. A second later, my bra unhooked before Coot's heat blanketed my back, sans his top as well.

I ended up lost between them as they both worked to destroy the composure I'd managed to hold on to, hardly noticing when Jesse braced himself against the wall and lifted me to give Coot better access to my pussy. The instant I felt Coot notch his latex-covered head against my entrance, I tipped my head back, holding Jesse's gaze as his partner slowly but steadily filled me from behind.

The gasp pulled from my lips when he bottomed out was swallowed down by the man in front of me, then I was clutching at him while Coot gripped my hips and mercilessly pounded into me. One of their hands snaked down to play with my clit, and my already primed pussy didn't take long to clamp down as I came again. Coot's groan was followed by his own climax before he unceremoniously slipped out, hooked his arms under my thighs, and twisted to switch places with Jesse.

I was too far gone to appreciate their coordination, but I sure as fuck appreciated the way Coot held me open for Jesse, who buried his head between my legs. He was only there long enough to ramp me up past the point of no return before he straightened, and without even wiping his mouth off, he plunged into me, stretching me anew.

"Fuck, woman, I'm not going to last," he groaned, reaching between us to play with my clit in counterpoint to his rough thrusts.

I was already with him, my body overwhelmed by the sheer amount of stimulation after going so long without more than the occasional self-care session. I came again with a shriek, head thrown back over Coot's shoulder, pulsing hard enough to make it difficult for Jesse to move against my grasping muscles. As my body quieted, he pulled out, ripped the condom off, and painted my stomach with ropes of cum, his hand pumping up and down his thick length to milk every drop onto the stretch-mark-ruined skin, proving his point about not caring they were there.

"You're mine, Sevey, whether you know it yet or not." The possessive heat in his eyes shocked me as much as his actions did, yet it held me captive until he glanced down. My gaze instinctively followed his to watch as he spread his spunk across my abdomen and pussy. I was ninety-nine percent sure the man had just permanently staked his claim.

I wasn't sure how I would have answered him or addressed the agreeing sound coming from Coot behind me, because a fist beating against the door, followed by the unmistakable sound of Lochlan yelling my name, had my post-orgasmic haze disappearing in a hurry.

"Sevey! What the fuck is going on in there? Open this damn door, *now*." Had he not sounded a whole lot of panicked under the pissy demand, I'd have ripped a strip off his hide. Instead, I shot an apologetic glance at Jesse before wiggling until Coot let my rubbery legs go so my feet could slip down to the floor.

"Get dressed," I hissed, worried they'd get the door open and find us all butt-ass naked. "Oh, don't look at me like that! We're all adults, but I'd rather they not get my VP to open the door and find me like this. Hell, he'd have the remainder of my crew with him. I'm just barely okay with you two seeing me without my clothes on." Both of their expressions softened at my explanation, and they quickly banded together to help me get dressed first, the gesture melting my heart just a little.

As soon as we were all presentable, a scant two minutes later tops, I pulled the door open to find two very pissed off Boudreaux men. Their anger turned to surprise as they caught sight of my companions.

"Well, at least we know where she disappeared to," Gus muttered under his breath loudly enough for me to catch.

"Really, asshole? I'm surprised you noticed I was gone with the whores keeping you company."

Shock registered on both their faces while confusion settled on mine. "We turned them down. We didn't have any intention of taking them up on their offer. We were trying to be polite since your VP sent them to invite us to a private party upstairs. After you left, we helped your prospect man the bar until most everyone else retired for the night. Do you know how long you've been gone, or how my heart dropped when I realized you'd been gone too long without telling anyone?" Remnants of the fear Lochlan had felt came out in his tone, Gus nodding along behind him with his arms crossed over his chest.

Guilt ate at me. Both for worrying them and for hooking up with their friends after storming out of the bar. Though my upset had figured into my actions, I couldn't bring myself to wish it hadn't happened. I'd loved every second of it and was pretty sure the guys had too.

"I need to get back to the bar and close up. Sorry I worried you." It was abrupt and to the point, and while they waited for me to elaborate, I slipped between them and took off despite Jesse growling my name behind me. They'd just have to wait until I had the bar squared away for the night. I wasn't naive enough to think I was getting out of a conversation with the four of them; I just needed to postpone it for a few.

An hour later, the downstairs locked up tight, we were in my room upstairs, having that talk I'd fully expected.

"I thought..." I started to say, but failed to finish in the face of Lochlan's explanation. *Yeah it was pretty fucking apparent what I'd thought.*

"Now, don't go regretting what we did, Sevey. I sure as fuck don't," Jesse all but snarled at me. I glanced from him to Coot, whose face was a stony mask, and back to the feral man.

"I don't!" And I didn't, but I was also seriously conflicted.

"Don't fucking lie to me or yourself. The second

you realized they'd turned the offer down, you all but climbed outta your skin to get away from us." Fucker must have had a death wish in that moment because I was about ready to remove *him* from his skin, and from the way Gus and Loch were posturing, they had the same train of thought.

"Kiss my ass, Jesse! I'm not sure what the fuck I'm feeling, but it's sure as hell not regret! You think I'd have picked the two of you to be the first I screwed since those two knocked me up?" By then I was up in his face, albeit I had to tilt mine up to glare at him. Asshat didn't have the decency to slouch so I could stare down my nose at him.

His mask of anger cracked, revealing plain male pride and something a lot softer that bordered on more than affection. Before he could act on whatever he was thinking, cuz there was for sure something working in that brain of his, Lochlan intervened, spinning me by the arm to confront me.

"I thought you and the sheriff were seeing each other?" Loch's eyes searched mine, presumably hunting for the truth or perhaps waiting to gauge it.

I immediately denied it while wondering if I needed to have a chat with Josh or if Lochlan had drawn his own conclusions. And if they had thought I was dating someone else but they'd still turned Tanya and Nancy down... I looked over my shoulder at the two who had the barest hint of guilt about them.

"Did you two think I was with Josh too? Why the hell would you have sex with me then?" Something wasn't adding up. Gus and Lochlan weren't pissed, or at least not as much as I'd have expected, though it was enough to mask the worry and upset they'd quickly hidden behind their anger. And Coot and Jesse appeared wholly unrepentant regarding the fact that they'd thought I was stepping out on another man.

Coot wouldn't fess up, simply shrugging when I nailed him with a glare at their silence, but Jesse had zero issue admitting it. "All's fair in love and war, right?"

"That's not an acceptable answer, Jesse. You know how uncomfortable I was. Why would you think I was hooking up with Josh?" I pressed, wanting to hear the truth.

"Figured you two were keeping it quiet because he's the law and you're not exactly on the up-and-up. The man all but staked his claim that first morning. Don't see how you missed it."

"I'm *not* with Josh. We dated in high school and have sorta considered maybe giving it another go, but nothing has come of it."

Coot's head tipped to the side as he narrowed his

eyes. "He was your first?" I was saved from having to admit a damned thing by Lochlan changing the subject.

"What do you mean, you were uncomfortable, darlin'?" he demanded, tugging a lot more carefully on my arm than he had the first time.

Gus, silent but attentive so far, straightened from his place where he'd been holding the wall up, the intent to cause trouble plain on his face. "You had our agreement to pursue her *if she was willing*! Why the fuck would she have been anything but content to be between the two of you?" *Agreement? Oh, hell no.*

"Excuse you? Before you go tear their heads off, you wanna explain this 'agreement' you made behind my back?" Gus stopped in his tracks, turning wide on me as he became aware real flippin' quick that he'd stuck his foot in it.

"I'll explain," he said with a sigh, then his eyes hardened as he looked past me at the two I could still feel between my legs, which made the whole sandwiched-between-the-cousins thing a tad bit awkward, "First, I want to know what they did."

Annoyed with whatever bullshit they'd cooked up and executed, I was tempted to leave them to what would likely be an epic throwdown, but after what we'd shared, I couldn't hang them out to dry like that. "I love our daughter very much, but I don't love the saggy-titted, wide-hipped, and stretch-marked side-effects of having a baby." I lost half my mad at the gobsmacked expression Gus sported as he tried to figure out how to respond to that, but I didn't wait on him to sort himself out. "They made it damned clear they didn't give two shits about any of that. Now, make that agreement crap you spouted make sense, asshole." If *any* of them thought they were getting out of that explanation, they would find a boot up their ass real fucking quick like.

"When our unit was chosen..." Gus gestured between the four of them. "It was after rigorous mental and physical testing. We already knew each other and worked well together, so we're not sure if that had any bearing on why they put us together, but the military psychologists did a damn good job matching us. Maybe a bit *too* good." He paused after the cryptic statement, though after catching Coot and Jesse together, I could put two and two together.

"You're *all* in a relationship? I thought that was frowned upon, especially between different ranks."

"It's more than 'frowned upon,' and we're not all in a relationship, per se," Jesse offered. "We've been very careful stateside to keep our dynamic private, and more so overseas while on base. But a lot of our missions were solitary, so we could go months without more than radio contact with another person. Those that put us in the same unit had to have been aware of what was likely to happen—sans Boudreaux. They didn't hook up for obvious reasons."

The atmosphere was tense as they waited for me to digest the revelations they were drip feeding me. It wasn't an unwelcome tactic, but it left a dozen questions for each answer, some I probably wouldn't voice in case I offended them. Some things just weren't my business, and vice versa.

"How do I fit into this scheme you've cooked up? Am I supposed to be your beard, so you all don't end up court-martialed or something?" The idea didn't sit well with me, doubly so while I still had Jesse's dried cum on my stomach.

Lochlan shook his head before I'd even finished. "We're out now, so that's no longer an issue. Frankly, we'd like to put that portion of our lives behind us; it served its purpose. After years of being largely on our own with only handlers overseeing us, the camaraderie of what should have been a brotherhood fizzled out." A dark look crossed his face, but he shook it off and moved on to the next part. "Anyway, you know Gus and I were looking for a third, but we'd thought it wasn't going to happen until we ran into you at the rally. At that point, we'd given up on finding a woman that would take all four of us on. Instead of pursuing the type of relationship we wanted, we started looking at places to settle where we could live together, or near each other, to start our lives after retiring."

"Jesus, Loch, spit it out already," Gus grumbled, then did it for him. "We saw the interest you had in Coot the night we met, and again with both him and Ares since we've been here. We decided," he pinned the other three with a glare, "that if the opportunity arose, we'd take it. *Except*, we wanted to bring it up *before* there was any chance of you getting intimate with any one of us. These two here jumped the gun. Not sure I can be too pissed about it since you're obviously interested, but I hoped you'd be on the same page first so we didn't get our hopes up."

I sat with the information for a few minutes, and right about the point they started to fidget, I broke the silence. "So, to sum this up, you four want to stay a family unit, you're all fluid with where you stick your dicks, and you want a woman to round out the group so you're a quintet?" At their various affirmatives, I nodded my head. "Alright, well, I won't say I'm opposed so much as surprised. Honestly not sure that I can take on all that testosterone on a permanent basis, but I'll think on it." Before any of them could react, or stop me, I slipped out and headed home, feeling a bit dazed at their proposition.

If I hot-footed it like the devil himself was after me, well, I didn't think anyone could blame me. *Aunt Flo is never gonna believe this shit.* I *don't believe this shit.*

Chapter Nine

Halloween Night

I'd spent the last few days doing my best to avoid any conversation involving me and the four men I was drawn to more and more as time passed. Surprisingly, or maybe not so much considering who she was, Aunt Flo didn't have a problem with their proposal. When I listed the cons men generally had, she blew most of them right out of the water. And I had to admit, she wasn't wrong.

They all picked up after themselves as far as I could tell, had good hygiene, were able and willing to fix just about anything, and they were protective as all get out. Especially regarding Opal who already loved her dads and uncles to pieces. Hence the escort for trick-or-treating being a deadly quad of bikers. It was the first time Lochlan and Gus would be in public with me and Opal in such a blatant manner, and I fully expected to have a dozen questions about it, something I'd likely have to get used to if I decided to pursue a relationship with all of them. Though that might have been more of a foregone conclusion after Jesse marked me.

Which brought up the subject of Josh, who I'd pinned down this morning. He had admitted he might have suggested that we were an item when he saw the interest the guys held for me. That discussion led to an argument that didn't end well, and I wasn't sure if he even still considered us friends after I gently but firmly put him in that category.

My heartfelt sigh as I loaded Opal up in the sidecar on the trike I'd bought just for the occasions she could come along was loud enough for her to pick up on.

"Why my mama sad?" She peered up at me with those eyes that looked so much like her daddies', then I was sighing for a whole different reason. One that I used as I strapped on her little helmet that matched mine.

"I was just thinking of all the boys your dads and

uncles are going to scare and run off when you're older."

"What about girls?"

I just shook my head at her question and changed the subject, going over our safety protocol again. There was no way I was going to try to explain to a two-year-old that her daddies would be after the boys to keep them from defiling or knocking up their little girl, so they'd probably whole-heartedly welcome a girlfriend instead.

Speaking of daddies, they tooled up on their choppers with Jesse and Coot right behind them. It took less than two minutes for Lochlan to bring up the safety of the sidecar.

"We're fine, Loch, I promise. We don't take her out in the middle of a group or at the end of one in case anything happens, so she wouldn't be in a pile-up. Plus, the speed limit on the frontage road into town is thirty-five, and the deer tend to run away from the noise of motorcycles, not toward them." Right about then, Aunt Flo pulled up, ready to lead the way, effectively putting an end to the discussion when Coot noticed her license plate.

"Does that say what I think it does?" he murmured to Lochlan, who followed his line of sight. I grinned at the raised eyebrows. I always got a kick out of people's reactions, and so did Aunt Flo for that matter.

A few minutes later, after we made sure we had everything, Opal and I pulled out behind my aunt's shiny red roadster with its vanity plate reading 'The Rag,' heading into town for what would surely be an interesting night of candy collecting.

The guys were helping Opal separate the loot as my aunt and I watched on in amusement. Turned out, Jesse had a massive sweet tooth for hard candy and kept getting on the wrong end of a toddler every time he tried to talk her into letting him have a piece. As contrary as the other women in her family, she only gave one up when he quit asking. At first, the others gave him shit, but when they saw how serious both him and Opal were about the exchange, I think we all realized they'd bonded a bit more. Without hesitation, my daughter climbed into Jesse's lap and held out the wrapped sweet for him to take.

Some uncomfortable throat clearing came from the others, drawing my eye to the men that were studiously trying to stay tough in the face of such adorableness. Heart filled with joy, I watched on while Gus and Loch got to share one of their first moments that I'd been fortunate to have the whole of her life.

As I was trying not to get sappy, the doorbell rang, causing a trickle of trepidation to slither down my spine. No one would be coming over this late without calling, not unless it were an emergency. Or worse. Club life was fairly tame out here, but violence wasn't completely out of the norm, and when you brought in the kind of money required of a Lipstick and Leather chapter, it drew all kinds of people in. Some great, then others quite the opposite.

I'd barely shared a look with Aunt Flo, who put herself between Opal and the doorway, when Gus and Lochlan picked up on our unease and headed in opposite directions—one for the front door and one for the back. With a jerk of Jesse's head, Coot took up the place next to my aunt, leaving both her and me staring in shock at the overkill. The doorbell went off again before a hard knocking sounded, prompting me to move from my place.

"You know, you guys are all sweet and shit, then you do something like this to remind me you're not at all harmless." My muttering was met with shrugs by both men and an askance glance from my aunt. Apparently, she didn't agree with my assessment, and I was fairly certain it was the first part that she disagreed with. Calling out ahead of myself before Lochlan scared the snot out of someone, I stalked in his direction. I was cautious, concerned about who was at the door, but these men were downright paranoid.

The instant I saw who Loch was talking to, anxiety filled me. There was no good reason for Josh to be standing in my doorway. Either something was very wrong, or he'd stopped by for a social call at an altogether inappropriate time. Since he was wearing his uniform, I braced for bad news, but I never dreamed he'd deliver the bombshell he did.

He looked past Lochlan, making eye contact with me as I neared, and my heart sank at the regret I saw there. "Sevey, I'm sorry to come by so late, but I need you to come downtown with me." He swallowed before finishing, giving my heart enough time to start racing. "Doc was found a few hours ago at the pullout on River Road. You're listed as his emergency contact..." I thought it couldn't get worse, but it did. "I need you to come down to the morgue and identify his body."

The first emotion hit like a knife to the chest. One of my friends and club members was dead. Then the numb-laced anger started to creep in as I operated on autopilot and told Josh I'd be there as soon as I could be. I missed what happened after that; Gus was suddenly there to guide me back to my family while Lochlan finished up with Josh.

Trying my best to keep my composure, I quietly shared what I knew with my aunt who blanched at the news. She and Doc had hooked up a few times over the years. They were the definition of friends with benefits. I hadn't known he'd listed me as next of kin, but I did know he didn't have any family. He'd come along with Aunt Flo well before we'd decided to petition and join with a larger club, handling double duty as both our chaplain and tail gunner. He was sort of the male version of Aunt Flo, and I knew it was going to be a hard blow for the club, her in particular.

"I'm so sorry," I whispered as I pulled her into a hug. I felt her nod, then her shoulders began to shake as my neck became wet. Opal, never one to let her great-aunt or her mama be upset even if she didn't understand why, wormed her way between us until we picked her up and cradled her between us.

At that point, I think the men hovering in the background got just how close of a unit the three of us really were. And then they stepped up to help us navigate the loss of a friend and club member without trying to take over.

Chapter Ten

Staring down at the body of what used to be a dear friend, my composure started to crack. There was little doubt the gunshot wound wasn't self-inflicted.

"Who the hell would kill Doc, Josh? He never hurt anyone and would give you his last dollar if you needed it."

Taking a step closer, putting us hip to hip, he put an arm around my shoulders in a one-armed hug. "I was hoping you might have an idea. When's the last time you saw him?"

I ignored the raised brow from the coroner. Dude could kiss my ass. My friend was dead, and another friend was giving me comfort. I only felt a slight twinge of guilt that had Loch and Jesse not been made to wait out in the hall, I'd have likely been receiving the same from both of them. That would surely give judgy-McJudgerson a better reason to act the way he was.

Shrugging, both at the coroner and in response to Josh's question, I answered the best I could. "Late this afternoon. He brought a treat bag down to the club for Opal before I took her into town."

"And your guests? Where were they this evening?" he asked, not ungently and with a fair amount of regret in his voice.

I stiffened in his hold before edging sideways out of it. It might be his job, but jumping right in to pump me for information didn't sit too well. "All four of them came with us to trick-or-treat," I responded flatly. "Aunt Flo was with us, and I'm sure there's a dozen security cameras that have footage of us downtown. Look for the real culprit, Joshua. Neither me nor my 'guests' had shit to do with this."

Pinching the bridge of his nose before letting out a sigh, he fixed me with a steady yet sympathetic stare. "I know you would never harm a soul without just provocation, but I still have to do my due diligence, Sevey. As it stands, I may need to turn this over since our relationship is a conflict of interest."

At his underlying warning, I felt my face blanch and hoped the coroner chalked it up to the stress of the night. We weren't ready to have anyone poking around; the greenhouses, processing buildings, and storage facilities wouldn't be completed until nearly spring. Until we had our licensing approved and the smuggling wrapped up, we needed to continue to fly under the radar. Hoping to derail his thinking, I snapped back, "What relationship? Surely cops are allowed to have friends, and do you really think right now is the proper time to be bringing this up?"

His lips tightened until they pulled down at the corners, and I vaguely noted our witness' eyes bouncing back and forth like he was at a ping-pong match. "Guess I was mistaken in waiting around all this time. If you'll follow me, I'll take you back to your men," he said stiffly. Thoroughly chagrined, he turned on his heel to stalk toward the door to the morgue.

With a last glance at Doc before the now visibly uncomfortable coroner covered his face, I whispered to my friend that we'd find who'd done this to him. Out in the hall, Josh stood with his arms crossed over his chest, the vest he wore under his uniform making him almost as broad as Lochlan. Despite my sorrow over the death of a friend, it didn't escape me that I had a heretofore unknown type—bad boys with a hero complex that didn't mind walking on the wrong side of the law when circumstances called for it.

That didn't stop me from blasting my ex-boyfriend though. "What the fuck was that in there?" I hissed at him, cognizant of the surveillance camera in the corner of the ceiling.

In unison, Loch and Jesse immediately turned and cocked their heads to the side. It was sort of creepy as fuck, but it did have Josh turning his attention from me to them. They, of course, were the bigger threat regardless of what the other man might think. Or maybe he did know since his hands went up, palms out, a pointed glance at me to defuse the imminent situation.

Shaking my head at him, I headed for the guys and motioned toward the exit. "Do what you need to for your job, Josh, but don't lend stock to anything more than a friendship between us again without discussing it with me first." From his curt nod and clenched jaw, I gathered he wasn't too happy with my order, but whether it was me calling him out or firmly friend-zoning him, I wasn't sure. Either way, I hoped it didn't cause a rift in our friendship that we couldn't mend. Feeling bad all around, I offered an olive branch. "Sorry for snapping at you. It took me off-guard. After Doc... It's just a bad time. Keep me updated on what you can?"

His hard stare softened with his reply. "Yeah, I'll give you a call, or at least stop by when his belongings are released. We'll catch whoever did this, Sevey. Doc was a friend to most folks around here."

Heart hurting, I gave him half a smile and let Loch and Jesse escort me out to their truck. I had a meeting to call and bad news to break to my crew—if they hadn't already started to hear about it through the smalltown rumor mill.

"We're going to find who did this, Prez, and put them six feet under," Tank said, nearly echoing what the sheriff had promised a short time ago. The fury and sorrow Tank displayed was mirrored on the faces around the room, and his declaration was immediately followed by the affirmations of all present.

Fearing there'd be a rash of violence to be laid directly at our door, I tried to curb the bloodlust coursing through the members of my club, rapping my gavel on the soundblock until they quieted down enough to hear me. "Tank is right. We *will* have justice for Doc, but we can't go around blaming anyone without cause. You hear anything, and you bring it to me. You all know I've been friends with the sheriff since we were kids, and he's on our side. He's invested in bringing Doc's killer in too, so let's try to make his job easier, alright?" Reluctant nods and belligerent stares from some of the more hotheaded members didn't bode well for keeping the peace. The last thing we needed was strife between the club and the whole damn town. "I catch wind of anyone going off half-cocked, causing the culprit to go free or harming the innocent, and I will personally cut your tattoo off. Do you understand me?"

That threat garnered the attention it deserved, and I'd follow through and excommunicate their asses too, so it was a damn good thing they understood I was serious. Before dismissing the lot of them so I could go home and grieve with my family, I made sure they would all be available for the police to interview, directly sending down those that had seen or talked to Doc to give their statements. I was plumb worn out and ready for the day to be over. An emergency midnight meeting was almost unheard of, and I hated the reason I'd had to call this one more than any other.

I woke to the bed dipping behind me and immediately pulled Opal to me until I made out Lochlan climbing in on her other side. Sure enough, Gus murmured an apology as he snuggled up against my back. Last I'd seen of them or the other two, they'd been taking shots with Aunt Flo. I'd brought Opal up to lie down, my head sore from tears and lack of sleep.

"We locked up, and Jesse and Coot got your aunt into bed. They're taking the guest room downstairs. Hope you don't mind us bunking in here with you?" Loch whispered, tracing a finger across Opal's chubby cheek as he stared down at her, his love for her plain to see.

I didn't mind them there at all and told them so before going back to sleep. As I drifted off, I felt a weight lift despite the upset I still felt over Doc's death. Them being there just felt *right*, and I planned to see about making it a permanent thing, right after I planned the best send-off I could for my lost friend.

Chapter Eleven

Amidst a sea of black leather, Michael 'Doc' Brody was laid to rest. There still weren't any leads, but we'd all put that to the side to celebrate and honor our chaplain and tail gunner. I knew I'd have to fill his positions soon enough, but that could wait for another day.

I made my rounds and kept the party from getting too rowdy as any and all had been invited back to the clubhouse for the cookout. After the grounds were closed to members only, all bets would be off, and as the alcohol flowed, it looked like I'd need to make that happen sooner or later. Not to mention those with kiddos would need to go home or make other arrangements. I was reluctant to ask Aunt Flo to take Opal, but the club president taking off wasn't exactly proper.

Surprisingly, or maybe not so much, Jesse and Coot asked if they could take Opal home. A few of the club members had started doing keg stands, and I quickly began the process of herding people out. Since Aunt Flo was in the line to get tipped upside down next, I gratefully accepted their offer and finished my more pressing duties before leaving my crew to it while I took a break in my office. Which was where Gus and Lochlan found me an hour later, well into a bottle of SoCo. My eyes tracked them. They were still wearing their jackets, as they had been the first time I met them, and I had the urge to ask them if they'd trade their gray patches for red. Drunk might not be the best time to broach the subject, but I wasn't about to table the notion.

"How would you feel if I invited you to officially join the chapter and move into the house?" I blurted out, a tad more bluntly than I'd meant to be, but I wasn't at all sorry that I'd said it.

The guys were shocked into silence long enough that I started to worry, or at least I hoped it was shock that held their tongues, not them trying to figure out how to turn me down. Lochlan, as usual, recovered first. He stripped out of his jacket before going for the button on his pants.

"Uh, how drunk are you? I didn't ask if you wanted to have sex." My voice was wary, but my lady bits were all sorts of interested in the skin he was exposing.

"I'm not sober, but I'm not drunk either, and I heard you just fine, Sevey. Figured we'd seal the deal with, well, sealing the deal." His cocky grin was mirrored by his cousin, who shrugged and shucked his own clothes.

"One of you might want to lock the door if you don't want to be putting on a show for anyone walking in," I warned. At Gus' sharp glance, I explained, "They'd probably still knock, my crew isn't disrespectful like that despite some recent bumps, but with everyone drinking, they might not wait for an invitation. I'd rather none of them get an eyeful." And then I remembered neither of them had seen my post-baby body and was glad I was at least halfway to three sheets to the wind.

"You have about ten seconds to move anything breakable off that desk," Gus warned, turning to give me an excellent view of his bare ass as he flicked the lock on the door.

I wasn't sure they would even give me that long, but I had the big bottom drawer of my desk open and the few things on top of it safely ensconced in it as Loch rounded it to pluck me from my chair. The shriek I let out when he effortlessly lifted me earned a chuckle from both of them, but it didn't stop him from laying me out longways on the desktop so he could get my boots off while Gus removed my top.

If they noted my self-consciousness, they didn't comment on it. Instead, they worshiped each bit of skin they exposed until I was as naked as they were. It only took them a moment to situate me on top of Lochlan, who had donned a condom, and taken my chair. As he took my mouth, his dick pressed in and sank home.

"Is it crazy to say I've missed this?" Loch murmured in my ear while his length stretched and rubbed me in all the right ways.

"If it is, then I'm going to the loony bin with you," I whispered back, followed by a moan when Gus unerringly found my clit.

"We'll book a suite," he teased, then he teased something else altogether.

I instinctively clenched and arched away from the spit-slick, probing digit, then clenched again when it invaded my ass. The effect it had on Lochlan was instantaneous. With a groan, he picked up the pace, jackhammering into me from underneath, and with Gus keeping on with both hands, I screamed my release into Lochlan's mouth while he pulsed inside of me.

"Hold her up, Loch," Gus demanded as he

swiftly pulled me up and off of his cousin, only to plunge into my still-grasping cunt.

"Condom?" was all I managed to croak out with my face buried in the crook of Lochlan's sweaty neck.

"Got you covered, darlin'," Gus reassured me, working me back up by repeatedly hitting my g-spot.

Lochlan took over double duty with his hand, supporting me with spread fingers to either side of my clit, giving me friction with every rough thrust I took from behind. It held my ass up at the perfect angle for Gus to fill with multiple digits as he pounded my pussy until I moaned my release without ever lifting my head. With the boneless state my body was in, I essentially became a ragdoll while Gus finished himself off to a soundtrack of expletives. They came one after the other, each punctuated with the clap of skin-on-skin, and had I had more energy, I'd have given him shit over it.

I tensed as he pulled out, my buzz having worn off enough that I was very aware that I was sore... exacerbated by the phantom sensations of them still inside of me.

Debating sneaking upstairs for a shower before checking on my crew and making coffee, I was side-tracked by Gus who idly made a spot-on presumption—one that had me groaning and thinking of rigging up a chastity belt.

"Hope you don't plan on walking tomorrow, darlin'. We'll take Opal out shopping while you seal the deal with Ares and Coot. Better make it early though cuz we plan on keeping you in bed as much as possible for at least a week. We have a lot of time to make up for."

I hadn't considered not giving the other two the same offer, but I also hadn't realized it was a foregone conclusion. I was just catching up on what they'd already figured out—all four of them were as much a part of my life as my daughter and aunt.

The next day's festivities ended up getting put on hold when I got a text from Tank. Seemed my sergeant-at-arms was out showing a couple prospects how to check the fence line when he found the squatters had expanded their territory and were now squatting on my land as well as the state land they'd already been occupying; they'd taken out a portion of my field fence to do so.

Aunt Flo clued in right away when I strapped on my holster and demanded to know what was going on. Of course, I told her, but I hadn't expected her to immediately tattle to the guys with a bellow worthy of a man twice her size. To say they were alarmed was an understatement. They hauled ass into my living room wide-eyed and packing their own firearms.

"What the fuck? Why do you have guns when you're hanging out with my daughter?!" I winced as soon as the words were out of my mouth. "I didn't mean it like that. It was a knee-jerk response," I explained in the face of the anger and hurt coming from Loch and Gus. All four of them were quick to re-conceal their weapons almost before I could blink, but despite their nods, they didn't appear completely mollified.

Finally, Lochlan grudgingly let me off the hook. "We know she's been yours for a long time, and you just reacted, but until we know what happened with Doc and *why*, we aren't taking any chances with her safety, or yours and your aunt's. Besides, she's napping right now. We were trying to figure out if we could get one of those Alaskan king beds in your bedroom when Flo yelled the house down."

"Fair enough, and we'll discuss the sleeping situation later, but for now, make sure you keep those in sight or have a concealed carry. I'm calling Josh in to come along and hopefully kick these fucking squatters out of town for good. Tank just messaged that they've trespassed and destroyed private property. He's going to drop the prospects back at the clubhouse and meet us there."

The four shared a look as Aunt Flo gave us a firm warning to be careful then excused herself to check that Opal had stayed asleep.

~

"They're obviously using the site, but where the hell are they at?" I asked Tank after we arrived at the farthest edge of my property to find their camp set up, but missing its inhabitants.

"I don't know, Prez. They weren't here earlier either. I would have made them pack their shit up if they had been."

"Sevey, do you know where their main campsite is? I think we'd have better luck at sorting this out at the source." I knew Josh was only trying to keep the peace, and he'd ticket who he could, but I was still annoyed with his downplaying of the situation. If he'd planned on arresting any of them, he'd have brought one of the police department's ATVs and at least a deputy for backup. Could have been his way of trying to protect me; I hadn't told him we'd changed our pickup point for the last few shipments until our transition was complete.

"They're a nuisance, and I don't know why the Forest Service hasn't been up here to boot them out yet," I grumbled, but I climbed back into my side-by-side with the guys while Tank waited in his to give the sheriff a ride.

Leaning into the open-framed driver's side, Josh fixed me with a pointed look. "Have you notified the Forest Service that they're out here?"

I shook my head, but it wasn't for the reason he thought. After Tee had failed to get them out of the area, I'd figured I'd leave it be and let winter drive them out as they hadn't set up a permanent shelter, not one that would withstand the harsh climate anyway. It would have been better for all involved if they had taken off voluntarily, but I wasn't going to sit around and let them invade my land without repercussion.

"If you don't get rid of them today, I will. They're well over their allotted time if we're going by state regulations." He just sighed at my glare, but we both knew I wasn't wrong. "I also don't have anything to worry about out here, so don't spare anything you can pin on them on my account."

The not-so-veiled reference to the smuggling that used to happen just north of here and my lack of concern left a puzzled look on his face. Then he gave me an accusing glare as he realized I hadn't kept him abreast of recent developments.

"Jesus fucking Christ, Josh, don't give me that look. I've been busy, and you haven't been out to the Hideaway. I've only seen you once since the guys got here, besides at the morgue. Chill the fuck out."

He gave me a curt nod and stomped off to get in next to Tank while I started my ATV and groaned in irritation. Thankfully, it was covered by the loud engine, so it didn't invite further commentary.

Chapter Twelve

The main camp was less than a mile off, so it didn't take us long to get there. I was the first to stalk into the hodgepodge of canvas tents despite Josh wanting to take the lead. I probably should have let him, but, flanked as I was by my men, I hadn't cared to let him try to smooth the situation over. Of course, I promptly ran into two people who shouldn't have had their asses near the place, let alone be fraternizing with the squatters.

"Excuse the fuck out of me, Tanya and Not Tanya, you lost?" Not Tanya had the look of someone that knew they were in the shit, but Tanya had apparently gotten into whatever they were partying on because she just shrugged before winking at Lochlan. Blood boiling, I started toward them until Josh looped an arm around my waist.

"Sevey, they're not prisoners, and they're not what we're here for," Josh hissed at me before turning on his sheriff's routine. "I need to speak with whoever is camping by the fence line back a ways."

"We're allowed to camp, officer," a man, a bit older looking than me, said as he came out from one of the tents. "Just like we told the old man this one sent out, it's public land."

My brows went up at the news. The only 'old man' would have been Doc, not that he'd been ancient, but I'd never sent him. Tee was supposed to handle that. A sinking sensation hit my gut as I rapidly processed everything, while Josh passed me off to Jesse and demanded to see the trespassers. There were a half dozen people around the central campfire, but there was evidence more had been there recently. From one of the dirt bikes I recognized, I figured it was likely they were still around somewhere.

"They aren't here, went on a run for supplies, but I'll tell them you stopped by and need a word with them."

"They'll be having more than a word with the sheriff. Private property has been destroyed, and they've set up camp on it." Lochlan wasn't at all amused at the brush off, and he'd apparently had enough of letting Josh deal with it. "We need names and someone to come clean it up. Now."

The man only smirked, but I'd had enough myself, shrugging off Jesse's arm before pinning the nervous Not Tanya down with a glare. "Sheriff, I'd like to press charges for theft as well. We don't sell bottles of alcohol out of the bar, and we've recently had quite a bit go missing from the storeroom. Tanya is drinking from one of them now." And she was.

The woman had the audacity to roll her eyes before smarting off. "I bought this at the liquor store, you crazy bitch," she slurred. "You're just pissed one of those men you're hoarding wanted to fuck me."

Lochlan tensed, but I shook my head at him. I had believed them when they said they weren't interested in her or her friend. With a smirk, I pointed out the stamp on the bottom of the bottle when she tipped it up again. "You see that mark on the bottle? That means it's distilled and distributed to the L&L chapters only. You can't buy it at *any* liquor store, and you certainly can't buy a bottle of it from *my* bar." Looking over at Josh, I raised my brows in question. "Possession of stolen goods is grounds for arrest, is it not?"

With a sigh, Josh nodded and radioed in for backup. "While we wait, I need identification from everyone here, starting with you," he said, pointing at Tanya.

"Hey, I didn't fucking steal it! Bronco gave it to me," she insisted, finally realizing she was in trouble, then she turned and yelled for the man in question.

I grunted in surprise as that's not at all who I'd expected to be there. Then it dawned on me that unless he'd borrowed the dirt bike, I had more than one of my officers fucking me over. "Where's Tee? I know that's his dirt bike over there," I accused, going with my gut.

"I'm right here, Sevey," my vice president said. There was regret in his voice but resolve in his eyes and defiance written all over his posture as he came at us from the side, gun in hand.

Josh immediately called in the situation as he, and the rest of us, pulled our own weapons. "Put it down, Tee," he demanded while edging back to keep everyone in the camp in his sights. "Everyone just calm down and put the guns away." I highly doubted he really thought that would work, but regardless, I wasn't putting a damn thing away when one of my longtime friends was pointing a fucking gun at me.

"Sorry, sheriff, Sevey, we won't be doing that." My disbelieving gaze went to Albany, who was coming from the opposite side. *Did my whole fucking crew turn on me?*

To make matters worse, several of the camp residents pulled their own weapons, though they weren't pointing them at anyone from what I could tell out of my peripherals.

"Guys, what the fuck is wrong with you? Put that shit down!" I was busy trying to push my fear and betrayal down and figure out how to defuse the situation when Tee went off.

"What's wrong with *us*? You're the one that decided to be a dictator, *Prez*. Did you ever stop to think maybe some of us didn't want to go legit? You're pretty much the only one that can handle your pet project with the sheriff here, so the rest of us are supposed to be what, your grunts? I've done *everything* for you for *years*. Who took care of the club and bar while you had a baby? Who was *always* there to help you when you needed it? I didn't want to be part of your fucking women's power, bullshit *Lipstick and Leather* club, but I did it for you because you were convinced it was a great opportunity. And it was, I'll admit that, so I went along with it. But then you came home knocked up from a one-night stand with stars in your eyes about the man you'd met.

"I didn't realize there were multiples, though. Never would have guessed that one after all the times you told me to take my companions elsewhere." All the accusations and scorn in his voice pissed me off, but they also gave me a sense of guilt. He'd obviously kept this shit bottled up until something set him off. "I thought I'd gotten a second chance when your baby daddy died. That you'd eventually come around, and I'd be there. Figured I might have to compete with the sheriff, but setting him up with someone else should have been easy enough. It's not like he's been abstinent while he chases after you. You've just been oblivious to it all. But then here *they* come," he spat out, pointing a finger at Loch and Gus. They had his death in their eyes as they closed ranks around me, on high alert in an eerie way that lent credence to their former career as a special teams unit.

"You barely put up a fuss before you welcomed them and their buddies in, made it clear they were above me. *Me*. The one that was there for you and Opal when they weren't. So, when you poked at me for not clearing this lot out, because I have a life and get busy too, I ran to do your bidding—like always. Turns out, their leader here found out about our operation and wanted in on it before you decided you wanted to go legit. Planned to blackmail you into letting them stay in the back end of your property so they could take over the smuggling while you acted as their front. Seems I might not have had the ladies where they should have been when you were handing off a few documents, and they shared their knowledge." Tee paused to smirk at the man who, from the unpleasant glare he was giving the traitor, was just beginning to realize he had no idea who he'd gotten into business with. If my vice president had been so quick to turn on me without an ounce of guilt, and jeopardize victims we'd helped, the leader of their camp should surely expect the same treatment. "So, instead of trying to get rid of them, I struck a deal. I'd keep the supply coming, and distribute it as always, while I worked on getting rid of your men and getting us unaffiliated from the ridiculous club you talked us all into joining. Go back to how it used to be. When you weren't a stick in the mud, and we didn't have to give a huge portion of our earnings over to dues every year."

I think most, if not all of us, were shocked by the words all but tripping out of his mouth. He was a complete stranger to the dependable man I'd known for so many years.

"So you decided to fuck me over and manipulate me to get your way? Why did you drag Albany and Brandon into this shit, Tee? You know you didn't have to do this, right? I would have let you leave if you'd asked, or tried to figure something out if you were unhappy. We're friends, for fuck's sake." I was more than a little butthurt by their betrayal, and I feared the worst was yet to come as not a one of them looked interested in putting their guns up.

"Friends, Sevey? Really? I wanted more than your friendship, but I was willing to settle for it until you let these dicks all but take over." He gestured to the guys, but the barrel of his gun didn't move back; he kept it trained on Loch's chest. I found out then that I could be more afraid than I had been. I didn't think he'd actually hurt *me* physically, but the men were another story altogether. Hoping to work a different angle, I tried to appeal to my enforcer.

"Albany, seriously, is this necessary? I know Brandon was upset about the transition, but why are you here? Am I really so terrible that you need to kill people over it?" When he blanched and darted a glance at Tee, then back to me, struggling to keep his panic down, I felt my heart break. "You killed Doc, didn't you? Why?!"

I blinked back the tears that clouded my eyes as he spilled his guts. "It was an accident! I swear it was. He came out here to deal with the situation, thinking Tee was slacking off on getting to it. Found him and Bronc trying to talk me into joining them. There was a shipment being divvied up, and it looked really bad. He took off to tell you and I-I—" He shook his head and dropped the arm holding his gun. "I caught up to Doc at the turnout where cell service comes back in before you lose it again. He'd pulled over and had his phone out. I just wanted to talk to him, explain that I hadn't done anything. For whatever reason, he reached for his pistol, but I got mine out first. Tee found me a few minutes later... I didn't have a choice, Sevey. I didn't want to go to prison for an accident."

Strangely enough, I believed him. But at that point, it didn't matter. We could hear sirens coming up the access road from the opposite side of my property. A couple of the squatters that must have been hiding out in the tents took off with bulging backpacks over their shoulders, presumably to hide, or steal, the product they'd planned to move. With the imminent arrival of what had to be the entirety of the Charity Falls Police Department coming up the road, hell bent for leather, I couldn't say I blamed them.

"What the fuck?!" Tee yelled, redirecting his aim to the camp leader who shrugged like he'd had no part in their actions. I didn't think the man expected Tee to turn and fire on his people though. "You're fucking dead! Bring my shit back *now*!" One of the young men made it to the treeline, but Tee wasn't a bad shot. He managed to hit the other, who crumpled to the ground, screaming, while clutching his leg.

At that point, his action started a chain reaction of trigger-happy people out for blood. With Tee no longer focused on us, I quickly found myself relocated well away from the worst of it as Josh yelled a warning to the combatants. I missed most of what happened, though I fought against Jesse to get loose when I heard his cry of pain.

"Sorry, Sevey, but I can't let you go back there. It's not safe." He didn't budge an inch in the face of my anger, but he did jerk his head toward the other three. "Help if you can, but don't take any fucking chances. Watch the cops too. They aren't going to stop to ask who is on what side."

The guys followed Jesse's orders, carefully working their way through the tents until they were out of sight, but by then it had quieted down substantially. Wailing sirens, accompanied by clouds of dust from the dirt road, rapidly neared the clearing.

"I think it's over, Jesse. Don't make me wait while people might need help." My tone brooked no argument, and from the way he glanced in the direction the others had gone, I could tell he wasn't too happy to be waiting behind either.

"Carefully, woman. I mean it. If you get hurt, we're going to have words." He motioned for me to follow him. I wasn't an idiot. He was the professional, so I didn't give him a bit of grief over it until we were able to see the aftermath of the violence.

As reinforcements pulled in, I ran to where Lochlan and Gus, guarded by Coot, were doing what they could for Albany and Josh. I quickly turned to keep Tee's body, lying a few yards away, out of my line of sight. Others were missing or had been caught in the melee, but those that could were trying to help the injured.

"Both Boudreauxs are medics. If anyone can keep them alive long enough to get to the hospital, it's those two," Jesse murmured in my ear, then he urged me down into the space between Albany and Josh so he could take up watch in the opposite direction from Coot.

Albany wasn't conscious, but Josh was, and his eyes locked on mine as I scooted back to stay out of the way. He gave me a half smile, I assumed to reassure me, but there was nothing reassuring about the entire situation or the blood all over him. I was thankful he had his vest on, or I feared I would have lost another of my longtime friends in this fucked up mess.

At that point, more police arrived, and for a little while, it became more chaotic. Several people were unaccounted for, Bronco included, when it all got sorted out. I didn't have time to wonder about him for long since we lost Albany. My feelings about him were torn. He was a good guy, but he'd also killed a great man, and I didn't know that I could have ever forgiven him for that, not that it mattered anymore. Worried that Josh would end up dead too, I refused to leave his side until they loaded him up in the ambulance.

"I'll be at the hospital as soon as I get cleaned up and check on Aunt Flo and Opal, okay? Don't be going anywhere on me. I couldn't stand it, you understand?" I demanded, hand gripping his as tightly as I dared.

He let out a weak chuckle, then groaned at the pain it caused while the paramedics tried to shoo me away. "You couldn't get rid of me if you tried...or unless you sicced your man-quad on me." Then more seriously, he added, "I'm sorry about your crew, Sevey. I wouldn't have thought..." He shook his head and trailed off as there wasn't much more to say on the subject.

"Ma'am, you need to move out of the way if you're not coming with us," one of the paramedics ordered, giving me a stern look that I was sure had served him well in the past.

As Josh was loaded into the ambulance, Coot tucked me under his chin and wrapped his arms over my shoulders to hug me from behind. Slouching into him, I took comfort from his nearness and waited for the other guys to finish up with their preliminary reports to the police so we could go home.

"You okay, darlin'?"

"As much as I can be. I texted Aunt Flo that we were alright and filled her in with the bare minimum, so she's on alert. She said Opal was fine when I asked, but I'm not going to quit feeling anxious until I can see for myself. I used to imagine all sorts of stuff happening to her when she was tiny, still do sometimes. I'd bail out of the shower with shampoo in my hair just to check that she wasn't in any danger. Don't know how many times I woke up in a panic just to check that she was breathing despite the monitor that had an alarm." I ended my rambling and shrugged as much as I was able with him wrapped around me. Feeling a little silly about saying all of that, I clammed up and chalked my oversharing up to what had to be shock and a need to fill the silence. "I guess losing friends, Josh being hurt, and the fear that I, or one of you, would lose our lives has taken its toll."

He didn't comment on the catch in my voice. A few tears had escaped through the course of everything, but I'd largely managed to hold them at bay. I had a feeling that once I started, I wouldn't be stopping for a while, and I preferred the privacy of my home to have a breakdown.

"I still have to tell the club, and I don't even know who I can trust there anymore. Hell, I'm such a shit club president that I can't even keep the loyalty of my club or see that I've fucked up enough for them to betray me," I said morosely, a healthy dose of self-deprecation thrown in.

Coot's arms tightened on me, and Jesse came up in time to hear my last remark. The leader of their quad wasn't too happy about it.

"We're going home, then we'll help you deal with making the announcement and any changes. I'll personally vet everyone so you don't have to deal with any more shit, Sevey. And stop being down on yourself. No one is perfect, and you can't control what others do. It was only a matter of time before that man decided to try for a coup. Feel sorry for the friend you lost, not for the monster he became."

I knew he was right, about Tee anyway, but I still felt the sting of regret. The one that said if only I'd done this or that, it would have made a difference. Pulling from Coot's embrace, I headed for the side-by-side, holding the keys out for one of them to take. I wasn't in any sort of the right headspace to be driving, especially not with my vision blurred by the tears I refused to let fall.

"Loch, Gus, let's go!" Jesse yelled at the other two. They'd finished with the cops but were having their own furtive discussion. I couldn't hear them, probably something that was on purpose since their heads were together, but at Jesse's shout, they broke apart and hurried to load up in the backseat.

Chapter Thirteen

"No, no, no, no," I pleaded as the headlights illuminated my darkened back porch, the door standing ajar in its splintered frame. Dusk had fallen on our way home, and as I bailed over Coot to get out, screaming for my aunt, we came to a sliding halt on the gravel drive.

"Sevey, wait, goddamn it!" Coot barked, unable to stop me from getting the door open and hitting the ground running. The others gave me similar orders, but I wasn't about to slow down, not after I got closer and saw what I'd missed before.

A puddle of blood with body-sized drag marks through it.

The guys were hot on my heels as I barreled into the mud room, avoiding the blood as much as possible, and sprinted for the stairs with my gun drawn and pointed at the ceiling. Right as I started up them two at a time, Aunt Flo came from the hall, hissing at me to be quiet.

"Severine! You'll wake Opal. Hush, girl!" She was a mess of sweat and blood smears, but she didn't appear to be hurt.

I reversed direction, nearly knocking Lochlan on his ass in my haste to turn around. "What happened? Why is the door busted? Is there someone here? Who's hurt?"

She waved to cut off my rapid-fire questions, answering once I fell silent, waiting expectantly. "We had a problem, and I handled it." Sadness crept into her eyes, but she squared her shoulders before adding, "Brandon showed up, wanting me to let him in. I told him to go, but he ignored my warnings. When he started kicking in the door, I told him I had a gun... Opal slept through all of it. Little miss was fine when I checked on her before I dragged his ass onto a tarp and out of the house."

We all stood there for a second, and at least for me it was from shock, but after a quick nod, I continued upstairs, more quietly than before, to check on my daughter for myself. When I crept in, she was sleeping peacefully, her little tummy rising and falling with each breath, reassuring me that she was fine. I was tempted to pick her up, but I needed to deal with yet another traitor's death and get a shower before I went near her.

Backing up, I ran into Gus who was trying to crane his head to see into the room. "Here, quietly though, I don't want to wake her up," I whispered as I edged out of the way so he could peek in at her to get his own peace of mind.

Carefully closing the door after he'd satisfied his need, he shook his head at me. "I'm never going to be okay leaving her alone again."

I sighed and stepped into him for a hug before pulling him with me toward the stairs. "I imagine we'll all be sticking close for a while. It's hard to leave her *now,* and I'm in the house."

Nodding his agreement, he followed me out back until we found everyone else standing around a tarp-wrapped mass I assumed was Bronco. I really didn't want to see the damage, so I didn't bother to get too close.

"With the sheriff down, and almost the entirety of the police department still at the squatter's camp, we have to wait for them to call in the off-duty officers," Aunt Flo was saying as we joined them.

"So we're just supposed to leave him here until someone eventually shows up?" I asked incredulously. "I can't hold Opal while covered in blood. I don't want her seeing *any* of this!" I knew I was getting hysterical, but I'd beyond reached my limit, and the thought of not being able to clean up because my fucking *home* was a crime scene was the last straw.

"I'll call and see if we can get an ETA," Jesse offered, pulling his phone out as Loch and Gus flanked me to give their silent support.

Nodding gratefully, I waited for him to get through to dispatch; they informed him that the coroner and a deputy were on their way to remove the body and document the scene. They arrived a few minutes later and weren't too happy with Aunt Flo for moving Brandon's corpse. Pissed, she explained that his body was blocking the door from closing, and she couldn't just leave it open with the baby in the house, so she'd had to get it secured as best she could until help arrived. The deputy begrudgingly accepted it, not that he had much choice with it being blatant self-defense.

It was still a few hours before we could clean the mud room and repair the door, but we were all quickly cleared to clean ourselves up. Coot took a shower with me, finishing minutes before Opal decided she wanted to get up. Eventually, I made it down to the hospital where Josh was just coming out of surgery and received the good news that he'd almost certainly make a full recovery.

Exhausted and shell-shocked, I still had to deal with calling a club meeting. Word had already spread, and I'd received dozens of calls and texts that the guys were helping me field, but I couldn't keep that up for long. The meeting needed to happen sooner rather than later if we were all to move forward and heal from the loss and betrayal of our friends and leaders of the club.

"Hey, I could have handed them shovels and told them to start digging," Aunt Flo snarked the next morning when Josh asked her what she'd been thinking to move a dead body.

We'd just come from the club meeting, which had mostly gone as I'd thought it would. Only a few had wanted to leave, and I'd let them off with the reminder to have their tattoos removed, but the majority of the club had chosen to stick by me. I had almost expected them all to abandon me, so I counted my blessings that they still had faith in my leadership. When presented with evidence of their loyalty and qualifications, the announcement that the guys would be filling in the gaps only garnered a few grumbles. I thought that their demonstration to help around the clubhouse and their willingness to go to bat for me had also gone a long way to gain my crew's acceptance. All in all, the meeting had ended on a positive note when it started with such devastating events.

"I'm going to pretend I didn't hear that, Florence," Josh said, rolling his eyes at me. He was sweaty and flushed, probably from the pain meds and exertion of sitting up, but he'd insisted on hearing what he'd missed. Poor dude obviously hadn't gotten more than a whore's bath since he still had streaks of dirt and blood here and there. I chalked up the twinge of something that I didn't need to be feeling to the fact that I was grateful I still had my friend and loved ones. As if he'd picked up on it, he leaned in close while Aunt Flo went to the waiting room to relieve the guys from Opal duty. I didn't think she'd caught on yet that they were more than happy to bear the responsibility for her. "Glad you have them, Sevey, but if you ever change your mind and want a more traditional guy, let me know. I'll be at the station, trying to pretend I'm not carrying a torch and hoping they fuck up so I can get that second chance I was working on."

My mouth worked like it wanted to say something, but I was having trouble getting anything out. I hadn't expected him to be quite so blunt, but the pain meds and near-death experience were probably influencing him.

Finally, I just nodded and patted his hand, then changed the subject without answering him. "I'm going to let you get some rest, but I'll stop by later with some soup so you don't have to eat whatever invalid food I'm sure they'll try to serve you." I stood to leave, turning back to shake a finger at him. "Don't give the nurses a hard time, or I'll kick your ass when I come back." He laughed as I'd hoped he would, though it ended in a groan at the pain, which I felt a bit bad for, but with three bullet holes in him, he was bound to feel *some* pain, narcotics or not.

When I walked into the waiting room, I found Lochlan holding Opal and a broad smile on Aunt Flo's face. I had no idea what they'd been discussing, but her "Welcome to the family, boys," had me thinking they'd declared their intentions or some shit —in a hospital waiting room, for fuck's sake. I'd have facepalmed, but there were witnesses, and I wasn't about to give them more gossip than I was sure they'd already gathered from the rapt attention the guys garnered.

"Mama, here!" Opal squealed over Lochlan's shoulder, holding her arms out.

In unison, they turned to grace me with welcoming grins, and had we not been in public, I might have handed Opal off to Aunt Flo so I could drag them all off for some private time. As it stood, I'd have to bide my time 'til the little miss went down for a nap.

"You ready to head home, darlin'?" Coot asked, holding an arm out to me in welcome.

"Yeah, more than ready, actually. And maybe a nap too," I hinted, pointedly glancing at Opal who was once again content to cling to Lochlan now that I was within arm's reach.

Jesse sighed, then gave me a wink. "A nap can be arranged, but we've really got to do something about that tiny-ass bed of yours. It's going to be a tight squeeze to get all of us on it."

He tried hard to keep his lips from curving up at the audible gasp from the woman eavesdropping next to us. All I could do was shake my head and make for the exit before one of them, or Aunt Flo, said something else risqué.

Epilogue

One Year Later

Masculine moans drew my attention, so I paused at our bedroom door. It stood open just a crack, something I was sure was deliberate as we were typically careful to keep my aunt and Opal from witnessing anything too graphic. Plus, they were out for the day on a shopping trip.

"I can see your shadow, Sevey," Jesse called out, all but admitting the open door was on purpose.

"I have a surprise for you," Lochlan yelled, but the end was ruined when he let out a grunt, then a moan, something that had me opening the door far quicker than the 'surprise.'

We all knew that was code for his dick.

The sight that greeted me had the panties I wasn't wearing in danger of getting wet; Jesse was reclining against the headboard with a mountain of pillows behind him, Loch perched on his lap and impaled by his cock. With their knees bent up, there was nothing left to the imagination, and I even spied the base of one of the steel plugs peeking out from between Jesse's cheeks.

"You two did this on purpose." I laughed as I shucked my clothes off. They were all well aware that watching them fuck each other, or do anything else really, was a weak spot for me. Something about it just short-circuited my brain and relocated it directly between my legs.

Loch's smirk only lasted as long as it took for me to crawl across the bed and take his most sensitive bits into my mouth. He let out an inarticulate shout as his balls drew up, though they were unable to escape the gentle suction locking them between my lips.

"Don't make him blow yet, darlin'," Jesse warned. "You need to be riding him so we can get you knocked up good and proper. I can't believe I drew the short straw and have to go last." The last bit was grumbled, mostly to himself, but there was no heat in it. We'd determined that while Loch and Gus didn't care who Opal's bio dad was, it would be prudent to know for any health or legal reasons that might pop up over the years.

I'd been terribly anxious when the results came in, afraid one would be upset, but when I saw Octavius Boudreaux and announced it, they'd all congratulated him...then immediately drew straws to see who got to father the next child. I'd had to interrupt their shenanigans to find out who the hell Octavius was. Come to find out, Octavius *was* Gus, which had been shortened from Gus Gus after a favorite childhood movie. It was cute as fuck, and one of Opal's favorite movies too, but I was just glad the DNA place hadn't screwed up the test results.

"Earth to Sevey," Loch rasped, pulling me back to the present and earning himself a rare blush from me as I realized I'd been sucking on his balls on autopilot.

"Sorry," I managed, lifting up and wiping the spit from my chin. But I didn't immediately jump on his dick. Instead, I got up to retrieve lube and one of the many toys we'd accumulated—one of the more powerful palm-sized vibrators. After briefly teasing the metal plug in Jesse's ass with it just to watch him squirm, I handed it off to Lochlan and gave his oversized dick a quick pass with the lube. I wasn't quite ready for him, but that would change soon enough, and just in case he went off prematurely, I figured getting him into position would be the best course of action.

The instant I took him to the hilt, he settled the buzzing vibrator against my clit, his moan echoing mine as I clenched around him.

"Oh, look, Gus, they started without us," Coot drawled from the doorway. Tossing a glance over my shoulder, I found Gus already pulling his shirt over his head to join in while Coot rushed to beat him to the bed.

I couldn't help but laugh at their antics, but the two men under me demanded my attention. Loch gripped my hips, forcing me down against him until the burn of him bottoming out had my back arching in a mix of pleasure and pain. If my mouth hadn't already been open, my jaw would have dropped when Jesse took advantage of my tits being offered up, twisting and rolling my nipples in the rough way he knew I loved.

Rolling my hips against Lochlan while staring at Jesse from under half-lidded eyes, I lost track of what the other two were up to...until wet digits pried my ass open and sank in to stretch me there.

"Mmm...too much, there's not enough room," I

moaned out, but I didn't try to move away despite the overwhelming fullness in my pussy and ass.

"You can take it, pretty lady," Gus growled in my ear as he pressed his chest flush to my back. Unsure if I *could* actually handle it, I nonetheless leaned forward onto Lochlan, trapping his hand and the vibrator between us as Jesse moved his hands to hold my cheeks open for Gus. "If it hurts, I'll stop, but otherwise, I'm about to be balls deep in this tight ass of yours."

His warning was immediately followed by the head of his dick replacing his fingers, pushing in until just the crown had breached the resistant ring of flesh. The sharp cry I let out, muffled against Loch's chest, stopped him in his tracks, but I blindly reached behind me to keep him from pulling out. I needed to let my body adjust to the intrusion before anyone tried to move a millimeter.

"Hold still and add lube," I demanded.

"Gus, maybe we should try another time," Coot interjected, but I shook my head and waited for the pain to pass.

"If you scream like that again, I'm stopping," Gus warned before dumping what felt like half the bottle of lubricant down my crack. The guys gave various noises of agreement, but now that he was in and the initial shock was over, it wasn't too bad.

"I think it's okay now, but don't you dare yank it out if that happens again. It will hurt worse." At my admission of the pain his cousin had caused, Loch used his free hand to tip my face up to his, his dark eyes searching mine for reassurance. Finding what he was looking for, he dropped a kiss on my lips at the same time he clicked the vibrator onto a higher speed. The sensations it elicited turned the pain in my ass to something much more pleasurable, and as my body relaxed into Loch's, Gus slowly worked himself in in the tiniest of increments.

"I'm going to pull all the way out to make sure you're slick enough before I get the last bit in." Gus' warning was shortly followed by a strange sense of emptiness, but the extra lubrication he added paved the way for him to sink back in with a nearly effortless glide.

His gasp made me turn my head to find his features pinched and body tensed as Coot came up behind him, eyes focused on what I presumed was his own dick breaching Gus' ass. A moment later, Coot and Jesse were fucking Loch and Gus into me while I clutched at sweat-slicked skin in the middle of them, clenching around the cocks stuffing me full as I tumbled headfirst into an orgasm. Loch invaded my mouth with his tongue, taking my breath in yet another way, while they all did their best to wreck me and themselves.

I couldn't have been more content than I was in the midst of the men I loved, who loved me back. The future was ours, and I couldn't wait to see what it had in store.

Afterword

If you enjoyed, or even if you didn't, please consider leaving a review!

For more from the Lipstick and Leather Motorcycle Club World scroll to the end and click the link.

About the Author

Emma Cole is a multi-genre romance author covering everything from dark and light contemporary to paranormal and sci-fi. Almost all of her stories are, or will be, from the reverse harem subcategory, and none of them skimp on the heat.

Emma lives in the mountains in the Northwest US with her kiddos and fur babies where she only puts on 'town pants' when absolutely necessary.

Follow Emma Cole

Newsletter Sign-Up

https://www.subscribepage.com/emmacole

Facebook Readers Group

Emma's Author Stalkers

Do you like dark reverse harem romance? The *Dark Duet* is a complete, ultra-steamy, ultra-dark, contemporary duology!

Lark: Book One of the Dark Duet

Dark. Gritty. Taboo.

Brokenhearted and mortified after being dumped when she expected a proposal, Lark calls her best friend and roommate for a rescue. While waiting to be picked up, she ducks around the corner into the alley to gain her composure, unaware it will be the action that leads her into a trafficking syndicate.

Kidnapped, along with her best friend, Lark wakes up to find herself in a cell with her friend, her ex, and her exes' partner, where they are forced to submit or become casualties of circumstance. They must stick together and comply—making the best they can out of a terrible situation to survive.

Stripped of all dignity and choice, will Lark make it out alive? If she does, what will be left of her?

Read Lark Here

The Degradation of Shelby Ann borders on pitch black erotic horror, so heed the warnings with this one!

The Degradation of Shelby Ann
Twisted Love: Book One

He was dark and handsome; charming, older, and rich.

She was the young and pretty girl, infatuated with a suave man who didn't exist.

Leaving home and burning her bridges, Shelby Ann was cocooned in the gloss of high society— the devil in a suit at her side. But beyond acquiring the skill and poise to pull off being a trophy wife, she would discover that all is not as it seemed.

With the honeymoon over, the dirt and grime

seeped through the loving facade to reveal the monsters that lie beneath.

Dark and depraved, this series will twist in ways you won't see coming to reveal an anti-hero in disguise, dirty deeds in plain sight, and shocking secrets that will leave you cringing inside.

18+ for mature content. RH as the series progresses (this is a slow-build). Warning: dark content, graphic/explicit scenes, violence, death, abuse, gaslighting, drug use, dub/noncon, multiple gender pairings, relationship dynamics that may push your boundaries of what's right and wrong, plus some things I won't spoil yet, but aren't for anyone with reading restrictions.

Read *The Degradation of Shelby Ann* Here

Looking for something a bit lighter? Here's a sneak peek at the *Remington Carter Series,* a complete, steamy, college contemporary, reverse harem romance!

Echoes: Book One

When well-laid plans for college went awry, twenty-year-old Remi took it in stride. With events beyond her control taking place and familial responsibility to fulfill, she did the best she could and waited patiently for her turn.

Now, two years later and back on track, albeit a little later than she'd hoped, things are finally looking up. That is, until an unforeseen circumstance arises. A flooding in her dorm building has put her into a unique situation that could be just the push she needs to take a chance on the up-and-coming football star that has taken a serious interest in her.

With elements from her past coming back for round two, will Remi be able to juggle it all?

Find out in this first installment of the Remington Carter Series.

NA 18+ due to content.

Excerpt from Echoes © Emma Cole 2019

I could barely see through the fogged-over glass of the shower, but what was going on was unmistakable. Forgetting that I was pissed a nanosecond ago, now I was rapt with attention on the show in the shower. My pulse was instantly through the roof, and lady town announced with fireworks that she's open for business.

Eli had one hand braced on the wall while the other was fisted around the length between his legs.

And holy cannoli, he was packing.

I'm going to have to plan for that.

Not that I was exactly sure what planning would entail to make that fit, and while I had a few good ideas, that's what Google was made for.

Eli's hand was moving rapidly from base to tip, and his hips were pumping up to meet each downward stroke. His own hand didn't close all the way around his thickness. As he picked up the pace, he started panting between moans.

I knew as soon as I realized he wasn't with anyone else that I should have turned around and left, giving him his privacy.

I'm not sure how I would feel if it had been the other way around.

Oddly, I found I was more turned on than off at the thought of Eli watching me the way I was watching him. As I continued to stare, Eli threw his head back and found his release. He straightened up from his slump against the wall, and I turned to go. I couldn't let him find me watching like a creeper.

Continue Reading *Echoes* Here

Dark Reverse Harem Books

Bad Habits Duology

No Good Deed

No Bad Deed

Twisted Love Series

The Degradation of Shelby Ann

Dark Duet

Lark

Nightingale

College Contemporary Reverse Harem

Remington Carter Series

Echoes

Requiem

Clarity

Resonance

Dark Paranormal Reverse Harem

Blackbriar Academy

The Order: Hit and Run

The Order: Ascension

(Coming soon)

Order of the Wraith

Avarice: House of Mustelid (Wicked Reform School)

Sci-fi/Alien Rom-Com

Alie and the Cosmic Convicts (standalone)

Reverse Harem Motorcycle Romance

Sevyn (standalone)

Lipstick & Leather Motorcycle Club World

www.ingramcontent.com/pod-product-compliance
Lightning Source LLC
La Vergne TN
LVHW041217150826
845673LV00001B/439

* 9 7 9 8 8 4 7 7 5 2 6 5 7 *